Contents

Characters

Nat Marley: New York private investigator.
Stella Delgado: Nat Marley's personal assistant.
Captain Oldenberg: detective with the New York Police Department (NYPD).
Joe Blaney: colleague of Nat Marley, ex-NYPD.
Ed Winchester: journalist on the *Daily News*.
Lena Rosenthal: Nat Marley's lawyer.
Robert Lake: President of Lake Software.
Angela Lake: Robert Lake's wife.
Tommy Lam: professional criminal.
Gloria: receptionist in Marley's building.

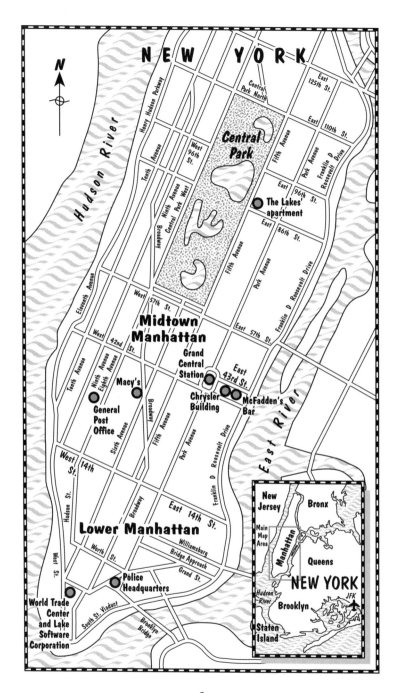

N E W   Y O R K

Central Park

Midtown Manhattan

Lower Manhattan

Hudson River

East River

The Lakes' apartment

Grand Central Station

Chrysler Building

McFadden's Bar

Macy's

General Post Office

Police Headquarters

World Trade Center and Lake Software Corporation

NEW YORK

New Jersey

Bronx

Manhattan

Queens

Brooklyn

Staten Island

JFK

5

Chapter 1   *The client*

It was seven-thirty on a cold wet December evening, six days before Christmas. As usual, I was in McFadden's Bar, on the corner of East 42nd Street and Second Avenue. Most of the early evening Christmas shoppers had gone home, and the people left in the bar weren't the types who had nice homes and families to go to. Maybe that was why they were still drinking. But I liked it there. It was somewhere to relax with a few beers after a long day in the office doing nothing in particular.

My office is just around the corner from McFadden's Bar on East 43rd Street and just a block away from the Chrysler Building. If I ever make a success of my business, that's where I'd like to have an office. Seventy-seven stories of the most beautiful skyscraper in New York City. New York isn't all skyscrapers, though. 220 East 43rd Street is just eight floors and nothing much to look at.

The sign on the door looks important: "Nathan Marley – Licensed Private Investigator," but it didn't make me feel any more important right then in McFadden's Bar.

I didn't feel like talking to people that evening and nobody tried to talk to me. That suited me fine. I looked around. There was a new face in the bar. Someone very different from the usual tired office workers. An expensive-looking woman. People turned and stared as she walked to the bar. She ordered a bourbon, then took off her coat. She was wearing a short black dress which showed a lot of leg.

Not the legs you normally see in McFadden's. Thirty-something, with long wavy blonde hair and cold blue eyes. Around her neck was a diamond necklace – the diamonds looked like the real thing. So did the matching earrings. She was dressed as if she was going to a party. But this lady wasn't enjoying herself.

She ordered another bourbon and took out a pack of Marlboro Lites. I could feel the coldness in her voice from where I was sitting. Nobody offered to light her cigarette. She looked in my direction. I thought for a moment that she was trying to catch my eye. But then she turned away with a bored expression on her face. Why should a woman like her give a second look to an overweight bald guy in his mid-forties?

McFadden's Bar was quiet now. I stayed and watched from the corner. I didn't have anything better to do that evening. For a change, something interesting was happening. I was curious and watched every move she made. She took an envelope out of her purse and opened it. I could see a short note and a couple of photographs. As she read, her expression changed. That hard look was gone. Now she looked like someone who really did have problems. Suddenly she threw a bill on the bar and rushed out. The bartender called out, "Hey, Miss, don't you want your change? This is a hundred bucks!" She ignored him and kept walking. Now I was very curious. I followed her.

Outside, the rain was turning to snow. On Second Avenue, the signal had changed to "Don't Walk," but she ran across just before the lights changed. The street was suddenly a sea of yellow cabs racing downtown.

When I finally reached Grand Central I saw her for a

moment – disappearing behind the information center – but then I lost her in the crowd. I waited and watched for a while, but it was no good. My excitement for that evening was over.

*   *   *

The next morning I woke up late, as usual, and walked to the subway. If someone gave me a dollar for every morning I'd taken the number seven train from Queens to Manhattan, I'd be a rich guy now. As usual, I looked through the *Daily News* on the subway. A woman had been mugged on 42nd Street just around the corner from my office. All her money and valuables had been taken. There were no names, no details. I didn't think anything of it. These things happen in a big city.

When I got to the office on East 43rd Street, Stella Delgado, my receptionist and secretary, had already arrived. She knows how tough life can be in this city. From a Puerto Rican family, she grew up in East Harlem. I've told her she should move on and get a better job. The strange thing is, she wants to work for me. The truth is I depend on her. She knows how to use all the new office equipment and she speaks Spanish, a useful skill in this city.

"Nat! It's nearly ten o'clock and you look awful. What happened to you?" Stella asked.

"Too many beers in McFadden's Bar last night," I replied. "Anything in the mail?"

"The usual. Bills."

"Guess I'd better earn a few bucks," I said.

"You could start right now. There's a client waiting. She looks interesting, but wouldn't give me her name."

I went through to my office. There she was, sitting in the client's chair. Beside her was a large black bag. Through a cloud of cigarette smoke, I could make out long wavy blonde hair and cold blue eyes. She crossed her legs. I'd seen those legs before, the previous night in McFadden's Bar. Legs like those are hard to forget. Then she looked straight at me. I could feel the ice in her eyes. I was getting very curious.

"Good morning, Mr. Marley. I've already been waiting half an hour. You don't believe in starting your day early," she said.

"I start work when I'm good and ready," I replied.

She looked around her. "This office looks like something out of the 1950s."

The office computer, fax and photocopier were in reception with Stella. I just had my old-fashioned desk, a reading lamp with a green shade, an ancient typewriter, and a couple of filing cabinets. On the wall, a 1990 calendar. A good year for me: that was when I left the NYPD, the New York Police Department.

"So I'm old-fashioned. I like it that way," I said.

"Don't you have any manners, Mr. Marley?" she asked.

"I lost them a long time ago."

"Don't you take your hat off in front of a lady?"

"I'm going bald so the hat stays on. Keeps my head warm. I'm a very busy man," I lied. "Let's get down to business. Who are you and what can I do for you?"

I've seen a lot of life in my time. Often the wrong sort. Fifteen years with the NYPD doesn't make you feel very positive about people. Then another ten years trying to make a success of being a private investigator. This woman had class and money. Why was she seeing an investigator like me? And why had she been in McFadden's Bar the night before? In my experience, women like her usually mean one thing – trouble.

Chapter 2 *Jewelry*

"The name's Angela Lake," the woman said.

She showed me her card. A Park Avenue address. Apartments don't come cheap in that part of town. Neither do cards with gold letters. Then she took an envelope out of her purse and passed me a note. Was it the same note I'd seen her read in McFadden's? Expensive note paper. The handwriting was neat and careful.

Angela,

Life was sweet with you. But now I realize you were only interested in one thing – my money.

I've informed my lawyers I want a divorce.

I hope you remember the written marriage agreement you signed. Let me remind you about paragraph 15:

"Any gift received by Mrs. Angela Lake from Mr. Robert Lake above the value of $10,000 shall be returned to Mr. Robert Lake in the event of a divorce."

You looked very lovely in all that jewelry, my dear. But sadly, it's not yours to keep. I expect every item to be returned to me within seven days. If the jewelry should not be returned to me, you will lose everything, including that beautiful Park Avenue apartment that you now have all to yourself.

Your future ex-husband,
Robert

"This is what Robert's writing about," she said.

She laid two photographs on the desk. Both were of items of jewelry. But what jewelry! Enough rocks there to open a store on Fifth Avenue.

"So what's the problem? He's divorcing you and wants the rocks back. Why do you need me?" I asked.

"You have to help me. The problem is . . . I don't have all the jewels."

Suddenly the ice was gone from her eyes. She just looked like a woman with a lot on her mind. She told me the story of how a girl from Coney Island had met the man of her dreams. Robert Lake was rich, successful, and the president of a software corporation. It all sounded like a dream come true. He was ten years older, but the age difference didn't seem to matter. They were married in six weeks and set up home on Park Avenue.

"Robert asked me to sign all these documents. I didn't understand anything about written marriage agreements. I was in love and trusted him. I was happy to do anything for him."

"So what went wrong?"

"At first everything was wonderful. But then he began to have problems with the business. He spent more and more time at the office. When he came home he was depressed and wouldn't speak to me. He became violent. Look."

She rolled up the sleeve of her dress and showed me her right arm. It was covered in ugly black and yellow bruises.

"Oh! He did that to you?"

She nodded her head. "He's moved out now. Something to be thankful for! The corporation owns an apartment uptown on Fifth Avenue."

"What happened to the jewels?" I asked.

"My family has money problems. I had to help them and I needed the cash quickly. I couldn't take money out of the bank. You see, it's a joint account and Robert would have noticed. So the only way I could raise the money was by selling some of the jewels. The rest of the jewelry is in a black briefcase in the Parcel Room at Grand Central. That's the claim ticket. I want you to get the case and return the jewelry to Robert – personally. I don't dare do it myself. I'm terrified of him."

"Why do you want me to do it? Couldn't you get a friend to do it? Seems simple enough," I said.

She handed me the yellow claim ticket from the Parcel Room and a small key. "Don't you understand? I don't want anybody to know. People would talk. If I give back most of the jewels, then I might be able to keep the apartment. Otherwise, I lose everything."

"Once I've got the briefcase, what do I do?" I asked.

"Take it with the key to Robert's office at 1 World Trade Center, floor 105. Don't leave it at reception. Remember, give it to Robert personally. Understand?"

I didn't understand, but it wasn't the right time to say so. Then she did something that I understood very well. She took out her wallet and counted out ten thousand dollars in new thousand-dollar bills. I hadn't seen so much money on my desk for weeks.

"Is that enough?" she asked.

"More than enough. My fee is one thousand dollars a day plus expenses. Just leave me two thousand dollars now. I'll call you as soon as I've delivered the jewelry."

"No, whatever you do, don't try to call me. It's too dangerous. I'll get in touch with you." She pushed two thousand dollars across the desk to me. "Thank you so much. You don't know how good it feels to have someone I can trust," she said.

"Well, thank you. If you wait a moment, Stella will give you a receipt," I replied.

But Angela Lake was gone. All there was to show she had been there was the mixture of perfume and cigarette smoke in the air.

I put my head around the door. Stella looked at me in amazement.

"What did you do to her, Nat? I've never seen a client leave so fast."

"She just offered me ten thousand bucks to pick up a briefcase full of jewelry from Grand Central," I said.

"Well, she's either stupid, or knows exactly what she's doing. Either way, I wouldn't trust her, Nat."

Chapter 3 *Doubts*

A yellow claim ticket, a key, and two thousand dollars lay on my desk. No business card, though. Angela Lake wanted to make sure I didn't call. Why hadn't she waited to get a receipt from Stella? Normally, anybody who's just paid me two thousand bucks needs a receipt. That's standard business practice. Everything seemed unreal: the way she had produced ten thousand dollars and the way she had left so quickly. Why did it all have to be so secret? And why had she tried to attract my attention in McFadden's Bar?

I had an idea and picked up the phone to call Gloria at reception, downstairs in the lobby.

"Hi, Gloria. Marley here."

"Morning. What can I do for New York's toughest private eye?"

"Thanks. I didn't think you'd noticed. But seriously, Gloria, a client has just left my office. She's on her way down to the lobby. She's tall, blonde, and looks like a million dollars. I want you to take a close look at her. Just tell me what you think of her."

"That's funny. I can't remember anybody of that description coming in this morning," said Gloria.

Fifteen minutes later, Gloria called back.

"I've been watching people leaving the building, but I haven't seen this lady. Just how slow is she?"

"Thanks anyway. You've been a big help," I replied.

"How have I helped? I don't understand," said Gloria.

I didn't understand either. I started thinking about the previous night. How I had followed Angela Lake to Grand Central Station and lost her in the crowd. This lady seemed to be good at making people notice her. She also seemed to be good at disappearing. What was she up to?

The question was: what to do next? Before I followed Angela Lake's instructions, I needed solid information. I could smell money, but I could also smell trouble. There was nobody at Police Headquarters who I could ask to help me. But I knew some other people who might. One advantage of drinking in McFadden's is the number of journalists you meet. My first call was to Ed Winchester of the *Daily News*.

"Ed? It's Nat Marley."

"Nat! How are things?"

"Can't complain. Listen, I need some information. Have you heard any talk about the Lake Software Corporation? Any inside information?" I asked.

"I'll ask around. Why the sudden interest?"

"I can't explain right now. I'm not even sure myself," I said.

"You're a man of mystery, Nat. I'll see what I can find."

My next call was to an old NYPD colleague, Joe Blaney, an old-fashioned, Irish-American cop, now retired. A fit active man in his early sixties, Joe was always available to help out with any investigation work I was doing. I gave him instructions to go to Macy's and buy a black briefcase. Nothing too expensive, but it had to have a lock and key.

"Sure," said Joe. "Are you going into business?"

"Funny guy!" I said. "Then put the receipt in it, lock it and take it to the Parcel Room at Grand Central. Check it in, then bring me the claim ticket and key."

"You crazy, boss? Why check in an empty case?"

"Trust me, Joe. Just do it."

Now I wanted to hide Angela Lake's key and claim ticket. If these items meant possible trouble, I thought it would be safer if they were out of anybody's reach for a while. What better hiding place than the U.S. mail? It can take a day or two for a letter to get from the east side of Manhattan to the west. And the Christmas mail wouldn't make it any quicker. I asked Stella to put the key and claim ticket in a small package and address it to me, c/o General Delivery, General Post Office, Eighth Avenue, NY 10001.

Just then Stella put a call through. It was Ed Winchester from the *Daily News*.

"Nat, I've been asking around. I don't have anything definite yet, but I've heard talk. People say that Lake Software has money problems. We're talking millions of dollars here. They put a lot of money into the development of a new product: a completely secure Internet trading system. You know the sort of thing I mean? A system that guarantees the security of your credit card numbers when you buy something through the Internet. That way you don't wake up to find someone's cleaned out your bank account. Anyway, another company – a competitor – Osaka Net got there first with a cheaper and better system, leaving Lake Software with a new product nobody wants to buy."

"You don't need to give me all the details, Ed. What I want is the big picture. Lake Software is in trouble, right?"

"People are saying deep trouble, but we don't know how deep," replied Ed.

Stella came in and was all smiles. She had just been out to mail the package.

"Guess what I've remembered, Nat?"

"Surprise me," I said.

"Anybody coming in or out of this building is taped by the security cameras. The film is stored on the security computer system. If you have permission from security, you can download it from the internal network and watch it on your own computer."

"Well, what are you waiting for, Stella? Find me Angela Lake . . ."

*   *   *

An hour later Stella came back with a puzzled expression.

"Nat?" she asked. "Describe Angela Lake to me again."

"Difficult to forget her. Thirty-something, slim, blonde, tall, wearing a black coat."

"The funny thing is, there's nobody of that description on the videotape," said Stella. "Gloria didn't see her enter or leave. But I've found something. Come with me and have a look."

Stella rewound the video until the clock on it read 9:20 AM, and pointed at a tall woman with long black hair and a backpack, wearing jeans and sneakers. She then moved the video on to 10:30 AM. The same woman with the backpack was leaving. Each time, the woman was looking down at the floor, as if to avoid the camera lens. And each time, Gloria was busy with people at reception.

"That could be our woman," continued Stella. "She

looks about the right height and build. And our client got to the office at nine-thirty and left at ten-twenty."

"So if that is her, that would give her time to find the ladies' room and change. And she had that bag with her. Big enough to take a change of clothes and a backpack, maybe?"

While we were talking, Joe Blaney arrived. Even after living in America for fifty years, he still had a soft Irish accent. In his time, he had been one of the best patrolmen in the NYPD, and one of the toughest. An ex-NYPD boxer. The sort of person you wanted on your side in a fight. He had taught me all I needed to know about staying alive on the streets when I first started with the NYPD.

"Boss, I got a black briefcase from Macy's just like you said. With a lock and key. And I checked it in the Parcel Room at Grand Central, with the receipt inside. Here's your claim ticket. What are you up to? It doesn't seem like your regular line of work."

"I guess it isn't. Joe, what would you say if I told you an expensive-looking lady offered me ten thousand dollars to pick up a briefcase full of jewelry from the Grand Central Parcel Room and take it to her husband's office?"

"I'd say that was trouble. Oh, I see, now. You're not as stupid as I thought you were, Nat."

"Thank you, Joe."

I told Stella and Joe what had happened the previous evening. How I had followed this mysterious woman from McFadden's Bar to Grand Central Station and lost her. I told them the full story of my talk with Angela Lake that morning and what she'd told me about her family and husband. The loveless marriage, the violence, how she had sold some of the jewels to help her family, and finally, how she wanted me to pick up the briefcase from Grand Central and deliver it to her husband.

Stella looked happier. "So that's why you asked Joe to check in another briefcase at the Parcel Room," she said.

"Yeah. I pick up the briefcase and see what happens. So far we haven't broken any laws. I want to find out what this woman is doing."

"Be careful, Nat," warned Stella.

"Trust me. Maybe I need a little excitement. Anyway, it'll make a change from doing divorce work and finding missing persons."

Chapter 4   *Grand Central*

From East 43rd Street, it's no more than a ten-minute walk to Grand Central on 42nd Street. After the Chrysler Building, it's my next favorite building in New York. Amazing to think they almost knocked it down in the 1960s. But I wasn't there to admire the building. I had work to do.

In the entrance, there must have been about a dozen guys dressed in Santa Claus suits collecting money. I suddenly remembered Angela Lake's two thousand dollars was sitting in my wallet. Possibly dangerous. If I was walking into some kind of trap, the money could connect me with her.

"Hey, buddy," I called to one of the Santas. "What are you collecting for?"

"Inner-city children in the South Bronx, Mister. If we raise the money this Christmas, we're gonna build a neighborhood center. It'll keep those kids off the streets. Give them a better chance in life."

"That's good. I like it. Doing something for the community. Look, take this and keep quiet, will you?"

"Hey man, that's two – "

"I said keep quiet! Do you want a community center or don't you?"

"Thanks. You're a great guy." I didn't feel like a great guy. I'd just said goodbye to two thousand dollars. Maybe some kid in the Bronx would thank me some day.

I made my way through the crowds and went down to the Parcel Room on the lower level. It was a small office next door to the Metropolitan Transportation Authority Police Office. The time was noon and everything seemed quiet and normal.

I walked up to the counter and handed the claim ticket to the clerk. He took it and looked around the shelves. He returned with my new briefcase and looked up as he handed it to me. He stared at me and his mouth dropped open.

"What's the matter? You having a bad dream or something?" I asked.

He didn't reply but reached down under the counter. An alarm bell rang. He must have pressed a panic button. The Parcel Room was suddenly full of police officers. There were two guns pointing at me. Not very sociable.

"Police! Raise your hands! Turn around, real slow! Lean against the wall! Spread those legs!"

I knew what they were doing. I'd used the same words many times when I was a patrolman. I was quickly searched. The key and my wallet were handed to the plain-clothes cop in charge, along with the briefcase. Unfortunately, we knew each other.

"So who have we got here? Well, well. If it isn't Marley, the private eye!"

"How do you do, Officer Oldenberg. I just love meeting all my old buddies from the NYPD. Tell your boys to release me. I haven't done anything wrong. I'm just collecting my personal property."

"Oh yeah? We'll see about that, Mr. Private Eye," said Oldenberg. "Sergeant, give me that key. And for your information, it's *Captain* Oldenberg now."

"Congratulations, Captain."

Oldenberg put the briefcase on the ground. The officers gathered around, expecting to see something big. But they were disappointed with what they saw inside. Just a receipt from Macy's, with today's date.

"Is that what you guys are looking for? It seems an awful waste of time and money. Three officers to arrest me and one empty briefcase. An expensive operation."

Captain Oldenberg was not happy. "Shut it, Marley! You're in big trouble. I want to have a little talk with you. A woman was mugged in a doorway on 42nd Street last night, after leaving McFadden's Bar. You were seen leaving the bar shortly after this woman and you fit the guy's description. Sergeant, take Marley to Headquarters."

It was the first time I'd been in Police Headquarters for ten years. But they weren't treating me like an old friend. They left me to cool off in a cell for an hour or so before I received a visit from Captain Oldenberg.

"Good afternoon, Captain. It seems like only yesterday that we were patrolling the Bronx together."

"Enough small talk, Marley. I need answers. And if you don't play straight with me, I'll make sure you never work as a private investigator again."

"Sure. You always did know how to make friends."

Oldenberg handed me a photograph of Angela Lake.

"Do you recognize this woman?" he asked.

"Of course. I saw her in McFadden's Bar last night – about seven-thirty. And she was in my office this morning."

"Don't play games with me, Marley!" shouted Oldenberg.

"It's the honest truth, I'm telling you," I replied.

"So you admit you were in McFadden's?"

"I just said that. Are you deaf or something?"

"A witness saw you leave shortly after this woman left the bar," Oldenberg explained.

"So what?" I asked.

"This woman later reported a mugging on 42nd Street. You fit the description of her attacker. Her bag was stolen with ten thousand dollars, jewelry, including a diamond necklace and matching earrings, a claim ticket for the Parcel Room and a briefcase key. What exactly were you doing at the Parcel Room, Marley?" demanded Oldenberg.

"Just collecting my personal property. With so much crime in this city, the Parcel Room is the best place to leave your briefcase. I wouldn't want to lose my lovely new case. Cost me over a hundred bucks," I replied.

Oldenberg gave up questioning me and walked out angrily. I knew, and he knew, that the police had no real evidence. I must give money away more often. It would have been difficult if they'd found those two beautiful new thousand-dollar bills in my wallet. I couldn't have explained them.

Coincidences were the only evidence they had. It was a coincidence that Angela Lake and I had both been in McFadden's Bar and that I had left the bar shortly after she did. It was also a coincidence that we both had claim tickets for the Parcel Room. The police had nothing that could stand up in court. However, as far as I was concerned, Angela Lake arriving in my office was one coincidence too many. Whatever she was doing had been planned carefully.

Chapter 5 *Fact-finding*

I spent the next couple of hours reading what people had written on the walls of the cell. It didn't do anything to improve my education. I thought about my situation. They couldn't hold me without charging me. But what crime could they charge me with? Not being polite enough to Captain Oldenberg?

Eventually, at five o'clock, Oldenberg and a sergeant returned.

"There are a few things we need to check out. Marley, you say the Lake woman was at your office. Why?"

"Sorry, Oldenberg. Anything between me and a client is private. And naturally, I respect that special relationship between client and investigator – " I replied.

"Marley, give me a break and shut up. And don't leave town. I'm going to ask Mrs. Lake to look at a line-up. I think you'll enjoy the experience," said Oldenberg.

"What, so soon? I was just beginning to enjoy myself. It's been a pleasure to be your guest. We must do it more often."

"Cut it out! The sergeant here is going to take us to East 43rd Street. A Crime-Scene Team is searching every bit of your office now."

Back at the office, Stella was calm but looked as if she was under a lot of stress. I didn't yet understand why.

"Nat, thank goodness you're here. I tried to stop them but they've got a search warrant," she said.

"Relax. We haven't got anything to worry about. And by the time I finish with the NYPD, I'll be getting a personal apology from the Chief of Police," I said.

The Crime-Scene Team had finished emptying the desks and filing cabinets.

"Found anything?" asked Oldenberg.

"Nothing much except empty bourbon bottles. There's nothing here. The place is clean, sir," replied the sergeant.

"You've checked the filing cabinets and the computer files?"

"Yes, sir. We've been through the lot. Routine office records."

"So we've been wasting our time?" said Oldenberg.

"Not exactly, sir. Look at this in the appointments diary."

In the diary, Stella had clearly entered the name "Mrs. Angela Lake, 9:30 AM to 10:20 AM." Oldenberg turned to Stella.

"Ms. Delgado, could you describe Mrs. Lake?"

"Tall and slim, with long wavy blonde hair, blue eyes, expensive clothes – a beautiful black coat."

"Sounds like Mrs. Lake. Sergeant, is Mrs. Lake on the security video?" asked Oldenberg.

"Nobody of that description entered or left the building between nine and eleven o'clock this morning, sir."

"So, looks like you both have lively imaginations. The lady wasn't here," said Oldenberg.

"I'm telling you she was. I spoke to her," I replied.

"And what did you talk about?"

"I'm sorry, but that's private."

"Marley, what sort of game are you playing? We've

checked with Mrs. Lake. She was at her desk at the Lake Software Corporation all morning, and she has witnesses to prove it. I don't know what's going on here, but I don't like it. Once I find out, I'll have you in Sing Sing so fast that your feet won't touch the ground."

I didn't like the sound of that. Sing Sing isn't a place where you go sightseeing. It's a jail in upstate New York.

"Captain Oldenberg, that's no way to talk to innocent people. What does it say on the doors of every NYPD patrol car? 'Courtesy, Professionalism, Respect.' You've been rude to me, you're acting like amateurs not professionals, and have shown me no respect. You'd better get out of here before I complain to the authorities."

Once Oldenberg and the Crime-Scene Team had left, Stella poured us both a drink. One bourbon later she was looking more relaxed. Then she reached into her blouse and produced a diamond necklace – the same diamond necklace that I'd seen Angela Lake wearing in McFadden's Bar.

"Ow! It's not comfortable with those rocks in my bra."

Now I understood why Stella had looked so stressed.

"Stella! Where on earth did that come from?"

"It was in the filing cabinet. I was filing the bills that came this morning when I saw something shiny at the back. I found it just before the police arrived," she explained.

"Stella, you've saved my life. The cops would have had all the evidence they needed if they'd found that necklace. Angela Lake had half an hour alone in my office. That gave her plenty of time to hide it."

"Nat, this is horrible. What's happening?"

"I don't know for sure myself. The Lakes are trying to make it look as if I mugged Angela Lake and stole the jewels. They thought I'd be the fall guy. A poor innocent guy to take the blame. I may be fat, bald, and forty-something, but I'm not stupid. I was suspicious from the moment I saw Angela Lake in the office. There's one thing I do know for sure – we're involved in this, like it or not."

"What do we do with the diamond necklace?"

"Same as you did with Angela's key and claim ticket. Mail it to me at General Delivery, General Post Office on Eighth Avenue. Once it's in the U.S. mail, not even the NYPD will be able to find it."

"Nat, do me a favor. Once this is finished, just stick to divorce and finding missing persons, will you?"

Meanwhile, we had to do some fact-finding. And do it quickly before Captain Oldenberg invited me to Police Headquarters for another neighborly chat.

My first call was to Ed Winchester at the *Daily News*. He told me that the Lake Software story would be in the business pages in tomorrow's newspapers. At close of business on the New York stock exchange, the Lake Software stock price was dropping fast – or as Ed put it, "going through the floor." Ed promised to get me recent photos of Angela and Robert Lake from the newspaper's photo library.

Stella agreed to work late, and I called Joe Blaney and asked him to come over early with the next day's newspapers. We needed to do some thinking. It was time to fight back.

Chapter 6   *Evidence*

When Joe Blaney arrived we looked at the newspapers. Lake Software was on the front page of the *Wall Street Journal*. The corporation had put millions of dollars into their new Internet trading system. Those people who bought stocks had been optimistically expecting the product to make a huge amount of money for them and the stock price on the New York stock exchange had risen higher and higher. Now it was dropping sharply.

Just days before Lake Software were ready to put their new Internet trading system on the market, Osaka Net had beaten them to it. The Press had interviewed the presidents of both corporations.

Robert Lake, President of Lake Software, had told reporters that there was no truth in the talk that the corporation was in trouble, and was confident that their new product would be a success. Akira Takahashi, President of Osaka Net, promised reporters that their new product would, without doubt, be the market leader.

When questioned by reporters about the recent attempts to hack into their research and development center in Long Island, Mr. Takahashi commented that a competitor was behind a campaign of dirty business tricks, aiming to delay work on their Internet trading system.

When asked if there was any connection between Lake Software and the computers being hacked into at Osaka

Net, Robert Lake had simply commented: "Absolutely not."

What is it they say? "No smoke without fire." Reading between the lines, Lake Software was in deep trouble.

While Joe and I were talking, the photos from the *Daily News* arrived. Ed had done well. He had also included the latest *Hello!* magazine which included an article about a society dinner the previous Saturday night at the Four Seasons Hotel on East 57th Street. The sort of hotel where you could kiss goodbye to a hundred bucks with a few cocktails, even before you started thinking about food. Angela, in an elegant evening dress, looked like she'd walked off the cover of *Vogue* magazine. The same wavy, blonde hair and diamond necklace and earrings. She must like those rocks. Angela was hand-in-hand with her husband – small, thin and bald, with diamond-shaped glasses. He looked like the typical computer expert.

"I need another point of view. What do you think of them, Stella?" I asked.

"They're an odd couple. She's so beautiful, but he's such a –"

"Such a boring-looking guy. What's the attraction – his money?" I asked.

"I guess so, but I can't believe he could be violent. Remember the bruises?" said Stella.

"He wouldn't have the strength," I commented.

"There's something about her eyes. An icy-cold blue. I wonder what she's really feeling," Stella continued.

She had picked up the magazine and was looking through it. Her eyes widened as she turned page after page.

Suddenly she pointed at a picture with the caption underneath: "Corporation President Robert Lake relaxes with his elegant wife, Angela."

Stella spoke: "I thought she told you she was terrified of her husband. She doesn't look too terrified there."

The photographers had caught them inside the hotel, on their way up the stairs into the ballroom. Angela was waving. Her long evening dress was sleeveless. The skin of her right arm was smooth and white, without a single mark anywhere.

"Would you believe it!" I said. "Not a bruise on her arm. Either Mr. Lake hit her after this photo was taken or Angela Lake is a fine actress. This is where we need your help, Joe."

"You want me to follow the Lakes?"

"I want twenty-four-hour surveillance. I want to know everything about them. Watch where they go, what they do, and who they see. We'll need photos for evidence."

There was a knock on the outside office door. Stella left to see who was there and for a few minutes, all I could hear was the sound of conversation in Spanish. Stella was probably talking to Mrs. Suarez, the office cleaner.

"What was that all about?" I asked when Stella returned.

"Mrs. Suarez told me she'd found this in the ladies' room. She was wondering if it was anything important. I lied and told her it was my make-up bag and that I'd been looking for it all day. Nat, I think we have a Lake connection."

Stella shook out the contents of the bag onto my desk.

"Mmm, Chanel! Nice lipstick but nice price!"

"Good work, Stella," I said. "This could be evidence.

The woman we saw on the security video looked plain. Women in jeans and sneakers with backpacks wouldn't usually go around wearing one-hundred-dollar lipstick. That could explain the make-up bag. Maybe she changed and put on and removed the make-up in the ladies' room. There are hair clips here. She'd have to put up her blonde hair before putting on a black wig. Angela Lake had to get out quick. In her hurry, she might have dropped the bag."

After Stella and Joe had gone, I took the subway home to Queens. I'd had more than enough for one day. I needed my home comforts – some takeout food, TV, then bed.

The next morning was miserable and cold. It had snowed during the night. Dirty snow was already piled up along the sidewalks. Cross-town traffic was moving slowly on 42nd Street. Steam escaping from underground heating pipes rose thick and white into the freezing air. Today, there seemed to be an army of people in Santa Claus suits collecting money outside Grand Central. One of the army stopped me.

"Could you spare a dollar to help poor inner-city kids?"

"Would that be the South Bronx neighborhood center project?" I asked. "I hope this helps."

"Twenty bucks! Thanks, Mister."

I was feeling generous. I could still be in a police cell if I hadn't given them those two thousand-dollar bills. What's another twenty bucks when you've already lost two thousand?

Stella was already at the office when I arrived at eight-thirty. Unlike me, she looked bright and cheerful.

"I've been thinking about those security videos, Stella. Can you enlarge a picture?"

"Easy when you know how, Nat."

"We need photos of the woman we think might be Angela Lake. Some close-ups of her entering and leaving the building. It's the face I'm interested in. And print out any good pictures."

Stella had checked through the video and had two shots of the woman's face. As the woman entered the lobby she looked up at the security camera. For a second, her face was almost clear. Another shot showed the woman leaving the building. She was looking down at the floor and long dark hair covered most of her face. At the last moment, she looked around, as if to check if anyone was following and for a second, the camera caught part of her face.

"Enlarge the first one, will you?" I asked.

Stella enlarged the photo again and again but the picture was poor quality and out of focus. What could you expect from a black-and-white security video?

"Is there any way you can improve the quality?" I asked.

"Don't be too optimistic. What about that?"

"I can see it now, but not enough to prove that Angela Lake was at the office. So we've still got nothing to show Oldenberg."

"Hold on, Nat. That lipstick might have her fingerprints on it," suggested Stella.

"Sure it might. And Oldenberg could say I stole it when I mugged her. Don't worry, Joe might find something. Now it's your turn to go shopping."

"What? Christmas shopping?"

"I want you to visit some jewelers in real expensive stores like Saks on Fifth Avenue. You remember the diamond necklace? Find out what rocks like that would cost. The

Lakes have – or had – big money. I want to know how big. Take that picture of Angela wearing the diamond necklace from *Hello!* magazine. Make up some kind of story. Say you've got a millionaire boyfriend who spoils you, and wants to buy you a necklace just like Angela Lake's."

Before Stella left, Joe Blaney reported back to the office. Joe had made several calls to Lake Software, pretending to be a journalist wanting an interview with Robert Lake. The response was the same each time – Mr. Lake was unavailable. In any case, surveillance of the Lake Software Headquarters at the World Trade Center was almost impossible with their offices being up on floor 105. You needed a security pass just to get through to the elevators. And if you succeeded in getting through, any stranger hanging around the corridors of a corporation headquarters would certainly attract attention.

Instead, Joe was concentrating his efforts on the Lakes' apartment, which he had discovered was at 86th and Fifth Avenue. There were no records of a Lake apartment anywhere on Park Avenue – another lie from Angela Lake. Joe promised us some photographs by late afternoon.

Stella was back after an hour or so. She had spoken to a jeweler at Saks, who told her a similar necklace would cost about half a million. The Lakes knew we had the necklace somewhere and someone would come looking for it.

Joe came by later with some photos he'd just taken outside the Lakes' apartment, then developed. The photos showed a long black stretch limousine arriving outside the apartment and three Chinese guys entering the building. In some of the photos, Robert Lake was with them. Joe pointed at an elegant man in his mid-fifties.

"See this guy? He looks like Mr. Big. He doesn't carry his briefcase or umbrella – the other guys do that," he said.

"Most businessmen carry their own briefcase," I said.

"Now look at these pictures of the three guys entering the building," Joe continued. "Each time Mr. Big is between the other two guys. I wouldn't like to meet them on a dark night."

"They look like bodyguards. Stella, take a look at them. What do you think of their clothes?"

"That's interesting," she said. "These two guys are wearing exactly the same clothes. Armani by the look of it. An expensive uniform. Nat, I don't know if it's just a coincidence, but there were a couple of Chinese guys hanging around by the front entrance when I came back."

"I don't believe in coincidences," I said.

I called Gloria at the lobby reception to ask if she had noticed any Chinese guys around during the afternoon, in the lobby or in the street. In fact, she had noticed a couple of guys across the street from time to time.

"If they set foot in this building, get security to question them and find out what they're doing," I said. "They could be watching me."

"Really, Mr. Marley!" said Gloria.

I was now fairly sure that something was going on between the Lakes and our Mr. Big in the photographs. That meant that I was involved too. I thought I might visit my old journalist friend, Ed Winchester. The time was approaching six o'clock, and I thought I knew where to find him – McFadden's Bar.

Chapter 7 *Ed Winchester*

Ed was at the bar, where I expected him to be. There was a group of young reporters around him. Ed was doing what he liked best. Telling stories about the good old days of crime reporting. Or should I say the bad old days? Despite his sixty-five years, he still looked fit and active. And he had a full head of white hair. Some people have all the luck.

"Nat, good to see you. As you're nearer the bar, same again, please," asked Ed.

"OK, Ed. Still as thirsty as ever," I replied.

"I'm worried about these young reporters. Do you know, some of them drink water?" said Ed.

"I'm deeply shocked!"

"You know, there's no future for a crime reporter in this city. Not enough crime since the mayor cleaned up the place. Only one murder on the subway this year," Ed said.

"I see what you mean. I walked through Times Square last week. I felt perfectly safe. I thought I was in the wrong city. Not like the old days."

"What can I do for you, Nat?" asked Ed.

"Look at the guys in these photos taken outside Robert Lake's apartment on 86th and Fifth today."

"Hmm. They don't look like they're paying a social call."

"The same people called twice today. Take a look at Mr. Big in the middle. He looks like the boss man," I said.

"I think this guy's called Tommy Lam. I'll see what I can find out," said Ed. He walked off and began talking to a junior reporter. Ed asked him to get some information from the *Daily News* Building and the young reporter left the bar. I sat down and tried to enjoy a drink, but I felt too anxious to relax. When Ed came over to where I was sitting he noticed me turning my glass round in my hands. "What's up, Nat? Have you got something on your mind?" he asked.

"I've got too much on my mind. I may be involved with something big and possibly dangerous."

"Dangerous? That doesn't sound like the Nat I know."

"It isn't. I should stick to finding missing persons."

I knew I could trust Ed. I told him what had happened during the last two days. He looked thoughtful.

"What I don't understand, Nat, is the Lakes' motive. Why exactly do they need a fall guy to take the blame?" asked Ed.

"I wish I knew," I said. "The story's much the same, whatever newspaper you read. Item one, Osaka Net and Lake Software were both developing a similar product. Item two, Osaka got their product on the market first. Item three, the Lake Software stock price falls. Item four, talk of a competitor being involved in the hacking into Osaka Net. End of story – so far."

The reporter returned, out of breath, from the *Daily News* Building.

"Your Mr. Big is a guy by the name of Yee Ho Lam. People call him Tommy. He's the boss of an organization called Shanghai Computer Commerce. They've been operating in the United States for about five years. Their office is in Chinatown on the Lower East Side. Now here's the interesting bit. It's difficult to say exactly what their business is."

"Yeah? Go on," said Ed.

"The *Daily News* did a feature on the Chinese–American business connection last July," the young reporter continued, "and visited a number of businesses in Chinatown. Most people were only too happy to talk and pleased about the free publicity. Tommy Lam didn't want to talk or cooperate with anyone. The business could be a front for something else."

Things were starting to make sense. I thanked Ed and the junior reporter and walked back to the office. It was beginning to snow again. Maybe it was going to be a white Christmas. As I made my way along the corridor to my office, I could hear the phone ringing. Joe and Stella had gone home and it didn't stop ringing. I didn't want to answer it, but knew I had to. I soon wished I hadn't.

"Marley? Oldenberg here. Don't leave town."

"What a disappointment. I'll just have to cancel that Christmas vacation in Florida," I said. "Give me the bad news."

"Be at Police Headquarters, two o'clock tomorrow afternoon. I'll send a car for you."

"Forget it. I prefer the subway. It's cleaner and cheaper."

"We've arranged a line-up. We're going to find out who mugged Angela Lake. Sweet dreams, Marley!"

The next morning was colder than ever. It must have been well below freezing. The top of the Chrysler Building was lost in heavy snow clouds. Snowplows were still out on the streets clearing the previous night's snow, holding up all the midtown Manhattan traffic. At least the subway was running normally. Stella was already at her desk. She was surprised to see me there at eight o'clock.

"Stella, would you call Joe? We don't need to continue the surveillance. I know who our Mr. Big is."

I told Stella what I had found out from Ed Winchester at McFadden's Bar. She frowned.

"What happens now?" she asked.

"We need help. Ask Joe to come to the office. You need protection."

"What about you?" Stella asked.

"I can look after myself."

"I wish you *would* look after yourself," she said.

"Now for the bad news," I said. "Oldenberg called to say I've got to take part in a line-up at Police Headquarters. Two o'clock today."

"Oh no, Nat! That's exactly what the Lakes want."

The phone rang. Stella answered in her best telephone voice.

"Marley Investigation Agency. How may I help you?" As she listened, her expression changed. Then she placed her hand over the phone and whispered, "It's Robert Lake. He wants to speak to you."

I took the phone.

"What do you want, Lake?"

"Really! Such bad manners."

"Get on with it!" I shouted.

"I need to talk," Lake said. "It's important, but I can't discuss it on the phone. I would like to see you at my apartment. It's – "

"I know where it is. 86th and Fifth. Give me half an hour." I put the phone down slowly.

"What does that man want with you?" asked Stella.

"He wouldn't say. Wants to see me at his apartment. Says it's important."

"It could be a trap, Nat. Just keep cool."

"I'll be my usual sweet self."

I'm a great believer in public transport, especially when it saves time and money. I took the subway uptown to Lexington Avenue and 86th. Then a short walk across to the Lakes' apartment.

I stepped inside the lobby. It must have cost serious money. Deep carpets and expensive wood. The doorman was standing in front of a huge antique desk, as wide as my office. He gave me a cold look when I said I had an appointment with Robert Lake. He phoned the apartment.

"I'm sorry, sir. Mr. Lake doesn't have any appointments with a Mr. Marley this morning. A mistake, perhaps?"

"Look, I spoke to him less than half an hour ago. He told me to come up here," I said.

"Mr. Lake's a busy man. He gave me instructions not to allow anyone up to the apartment without his permission."

"Now look here, buddy. I'm losing patience. Just call him again, will you?"

"Don't call me 'buddy,' Mister!" said the doorman. "If you don't leave right now, I'll call 911."

I was angry now. People in the lobby turned and stared.

"I want to see Lake," I shouted. "And when I've finished with him, he'll be sorry he ever tried to mess with Nat Marley."

The elevator door opened behind the desk. It was Lake, a small, bald man with ridiculous diamond-shaped glasses. Angela Lake had to be deeply in love with his bank account.

"Ah, Mr. Marley, so pleased you could come," said Lake.

"You could have told the doorman!"

"A breakdown in communication. These things happen," said Lake.

The doorman smiled unpleasantly at me. It had been planned. Lake took me up to his apartment. Through the windows there was a view of Central Park and the frozen lake. It was snowing again, and kids were throwing snowballs and building snowmen. Just like a scene from a Christmas card. It didn't feel like Christmas in the apartment though.

Lake looked even smaller than he did in the photographs. How could this little guy be worth millions?

"You're a failure, Marley. That's why we chose you to be the fall guy," he said.

"You set me up, Lake. You and Angela planned this all together. She might be a good actress, but the two of you are just amateurs. You made it all too complicated. You couldn't keep it simple."

"Sure, we made mistakes, but we'll be the winners in this game and you'll always be the loser. I'm looking forward to this afternoon, when Angela picks you out from the line-up."

"Why me, Lake?"

"Nothing personal. I needed someone with a small business. The type of guy who had trouble paying the bills.

I heard about you from a colleague who was going through a divorce. He'd hired you to follow his wife. You were just perfect. Though you're not as stupid as I'd imagined. That trick with the briefcase. Very neat."

"Just tell me one thing. What's your motive?" I asked.

Lake couldn't stop himself. He was enjoying every moment.

"Running a corporation by the rules gets boring after a while. I want to play in the big game for the money, power, and excitement. The game is for real, and I get a kick out of it. I enjoy the sense of danger. I wanted to be the major player. Osaka Net was the only corporation that stood between me and control of the world markets. I didn't care what methods I used, or who helped me to achieve my aims. The rules are there to be broken."

"You've lost, Lake."

"It's not over yet. I'll be up there again, with the best of them and I'm not particular about how I do it."

"In real life, Lake, people get hurt."

"Exactly, Mr. Marley."

Lake paused and closely examined his right hand. On each finger, there was a ring with a stone set in it. Then, Lake took me by surprise. Suddenly he raised his arm and hit me hard in the mouth. Hard enough to hurt me with the rings. I could taste blood in my mouth and felt a tiny piece of broken tooth. I don't like being hit by guys like Robert Lake. I especially don't like being hit by guys wearing rings. I lost my cool and punched him hard on the nose. I felt breaking bone and plastic. It hurt my hand, but I hope it hurt him a lot more. I think I broke both his nose and those silly glasses. Then he surprised me again. As he got up from the floor, with blood pouring from his nose, he grinned.

"As I said, Marley, you're still the fall guy. We'll always be one step ahead. It's all exactly as I'd planned."

Lake pressed a button on his desk. Two of the largest security men I had ever seen walked in and picked me up as if I were a child.

"Everything on camera, boys?" asked Lake.

"Sure thing, boss. The fool fell for it."

"Excellent! Captain Oldenberg will enjoy watching it," said Lake with a satisfied smile.

I couldn't believe what was happening.

"You hit me first, you bast– " I began.

"Such bad manners! Haven't you heard of film editing? Captain Oldenberg will have all the evidence he needs. A videotape of you attacking me, and me trying to protect myself. The camera doesn't lie."

"Is this how you normally treat your guests?" I asked. "Don't bother seeing me to the door. I'll find my own way out."

Chapter 8 *Tommy Lam*

Downstairs in the lobby at 86th and Fifth, a smartly dressed Chinese man was waiting for me. I knew the name and face. Yee Ho or Tommy Lam. His suit was so shiny that I could almost see my face in it. There was a large yellow diamond in his tiepin. The same guy I'd seen in the photographs.

"How do you do, Mr. Marley?" he said.

"I was wondering when I'd meet you, Mr. Lam. What can I do for you?"

"You've done your homework. I'd like to invite you for a drive around the park," he said.

I noticed the two bodyguards in Armani suits and dark glasses.

"An invitation I can't refuse?" I asked, looking in their direction.

"Of course. I'm glad to see you're a professional. Come this way."

The black limousine was parked outside. Inside the car, it was all warmth, comfort, and luxury. The two bodyguards sat across the back seat and took off their dark glasses. Their faces were expressionless. Tommy Lam invited me to sit in one of the leather armchairs beside a mini bar. The car headed downtown along Fifth Avenue toward Central Park South.

"I'm very grateful you agreed to come for an informal

chat, Mr. Marley. I believe a host should honor his guest. It's an old Chinese tradition. So first a little drink."

"Large Scotch," I said.

Lam pointed at one of the bodyguards, who prepared the drinks. The Scotch was better quality than anything in McFadden's Bar.

"The park looks so attractive in the snow. Enjoy the view and your drink, Mr. Marley. Pleasure before business."

We sat in silence while I drank the Scotch. Lam didn't seem to be in a hurry. The huge car turned right at Columbus Circle, and continued uptown on Central Park West. Finally Lam spoke.

"I understand your interest in the Lakes. I dislike the Lakes with good reason. They're amateurs playing games. We've been watching the Lakes. And I think you have, too."

"What's your interest in the Lakes?" I asked.

"Money. They owe me a lot of money." Lam took out a calculator and punched the buttons. "Five million dollars. The agreement was payment in cash or jewelry. Mrs. Lake has some valuable items of jewelry which I am very fond of. I've always been careful with money. You see, Mr. Marley, we are both involved with crime. You solve crimes and I'm the criminal. I did some work for Robert Lake. Skilled work," Lam continued. "It involved hacking into computers at a development center."

"Would this be the Osaka Net center?" I asked.

"Again I see you've done your homework, Mr. Marley. I carried out my side of the deal, but Lake has accused me of hacking into the wrong systems at the center. The fault was not mine. I carried out his instructions exactly. We hacked into their computers twice – a professional job I could be proud of. Now the payment is late. I need to protect my interests, so my people have been watching them."

Lam paused. "So, Mr. Marley, why did Angela Lake visit your office building on Tuesday morning with that silly change of clothes and hair?"

"You know about that?" I said, surprised.

"An obvious trick. She was easy to follow. And I also know about your visit to the Parcel Room at Grand Central through my friends in the police. Tell me everything I want to know and I'll treat you right. But if you don't . . . my colleagues have ways of persuading people."

I realized Lam was not the sort of guy to take chances with. He was dangerous. Lam continued in the same polite voice as the car continued along Central Park West.

"Violence is unpleasant but sometimes necessary. You wouldn't want anything to happen to Ms. Delgado, would you?" Lam said.

The bodyguards suddenly smiled unpleasantly. Then their faces became expressionless once again. I had no choice but to tell Lam everything – or nearly everything – starting with McFadden's Bar on Monday evening. Lam listened carefully as I told him how Angela Lake had tried to set me up.

Lam looked thoughtfully out of the window. "Well, there could be some truth among the lies," he said. "The Lakes wanted you to be their fall guy. That doesn't worry me in the least. You're a minor player in this affair."

"It's good to feel valued," I replied.

"What does worry me is the jewelry which Mrs. Lake claims was stolen. I'm not so sure about that. I also want to know what's inside her briefcase in the Parcel Room at Grand Central. I suspect that the Lakes may be trying to escape their responsibilities toward me. What did you do with the key and claim ticket?" asked Lam.

"Put them in a safe place. The U.S. mail."

"Clever move. The address, if you please?" Lam said.

"General Delivery, General Post Office, Eighth Avenue," I replied. I didn't have a lot of choice.

Lam spoke into the intercom. The car made a left after the American Museum of Natural History then headed downtown on Columbus Avenue. I was hoping the Christmas mail was as slow as usual. I sat in silence and kept my fingers crossed. After 57th Street, Columbus Avenue becomes Ninth Avenue.

"Stay on Ninth for General Delivery," I said.

"I thought everything was on Eighth?" said Lam.

"It's the only department that isn't."

The General Post Office takes up a whole block. The front on Eighth Avenue is like an ancient Greek temple. The back of the building on Ninth is quite different. Lam didn't know everything about New York. They put General Delivery on Ninth for a very good reason. Many homeless New Yorkers use it as a safe address. The respectable customers entering by the front entrance don't see the down-and-outs. Maybe that's why the Post Office Police Office is next door to General Delivery.

Inside the General Delivery office, two lines of sad-looking people waited their turn. Mine was the only white face in the room. Lam and his bodyguards in their Armani suits didn't look as if they belonged there. Lam wasn't used to waiting. He walked straight up to the window, tapped on it and demanded a package for Nat Marley. There were angry shouts from the lines.

"Hey, man! What do you think you're doing?"

"Who do you think you are? There's a line here."

The U.S. Post Office has its rules and not even Lam could break them. The clerk believed rules were there for a reason.

"I don't care who you are, Mister. Get in line like everyone else or I'll call security."

We waited ten minutes on the line. I showed my ID to the clerk who took down a pile of letters and went through them.

"No, sir. Nothing for Marley."

Perfect. I could have kissed the clerk. That would have been difficult with a glass security window in the way. I'd never complain about the U.S. Post Office again. I needed that claim ticket and key. I particularly needed the diamond necklace, and I didn't want to give Lam all my evidence. Lam, understandably, was not pleased.

"I'll be watching you, Marley. You try to collect anything from this office, and I'll know about it. Be at your office at ten o'clock tomorrow morning. We'll try again and again until I have that package," said Lam. "Take a walk to your office. The exercise will do you good."

I didn't mind. I preferred the subway to Tommy Lam's limo. I caught an uptown E train from 34th Street. I felt more comfortable in a crowded subway car with ordinary folks.

Chapter 9 *Line-up*

By the time I got back to my office it was almost noon.
Stella was anxious.

"Where have you been all this time?" she asked.

"Just riding around Central Park in a limo, drinking
good Scotch," I answered.

"No, seriously, Nat."

She looked concerned as I told her what had happened
in Lake's office.

"Oh no, Nat. He wanted you to punch him."

"I know. More evidence for Oldenberg. It's all on video.
Where's Joe?" I asked.

"He's just gone out to get some lunch."

"Tell him I want him with you all the time. Lam is
dangerous. Lake owes him money and Lam's not going to
wait. He knows about the first package to General
Delivery. In fact, he took me there to pick it up."

"Let me guess. It hadn't arrived," said Stella.

"Correct. Thank you, Post Office."

I had to be downtown for my appointment at Police
Headquarters with Captain Oldenberg. When I arrived at
reception, I was taken downstairs to where Oldenberg was
waiting. He was enjoying himself.

"The famous private eye again! You're a busy man. What
made you visit the Lake's apartment?" asked Oldenberg.

"I had a personal invitation," I replied.

"Not according to Mr. Lake. He's made a complaint."

50

"He's lying," I said.

"We have you on security videos. Shouting at the doorman and then punching Lake. I never knew you could be so aggressive. And that poor guy trying to protect himself. But we'll talk about that later. We've got a line-up ready. Sergeant, take Marley to the line-up room."

There were no windows in the room. It was painted a depressing dirty green. Waiting there were half a dozen of the saddest-looking guys you could imagine. Fat, bald and forty-something. All wearing cheap suits. The frightening thing was I looked just like them. They were here just to earn a few bucks, but I could be in jail for a long time. I was given a number five to hold.

We were facing a two-way mirror. Nothing happened for a couple of minutes. Then an order came over the intercom: "Number five, step forward." Silence again. I was told to step back in line. Two other guys were asked to step forward. Angela Lake must have been doing some good acting behind the mirror. Finally another order came over the intercom: "Number five stay, and thank you everybody for taking part."

Oldenberg entered. He looked even more cheerful as he arrested me. "Nathan Marley, I am arresting you for the robbery of Mrs. Angela Lake on East 42nd Street. Also, for the assault of Mr. Robert Lake in his apartment on 86th and Fifth. Take him away, Sergeant."

"Oldenberg, I know my rights. I need to speak to my lawyer," I demanded.

"OK. Sergeant, let him make his phone call."

The situation couldn't have been worse. I needed a good lawyer to get me out of this mess. I had done several jobs for Rosenthal and Rosenthal, a firm of criminal lawyers on Lexington Avenue. Lena Rosenthal was one of the best. Fortunately, she wasn't in court that afternoon.

"Lena, it's Marley."

"Nat, how are things?"

"Not good. I'm at Police Headquarters. I've been charged with robbery and assault."

"This is serious, Nat."

"It's a very long story. Some very powerful people want a fall guy," I said.

"I'll be right with you. Don't say anything to anyone."

Lena was there within the hour. I told her the full story, including my visit to Lake's apartment, and my meeting with Tommy Lam and our trip to the Post Office.

"You're smart, Nat. If you'd taken the real claim ticket to the Parcel Room, there wouldn't be much I could do. But the situation isn't hopeless. As you know, a positive identification doesn't mean you're guilty. People get confused. It's easy to make mistakes with line-ups."

"Apart from the identification, the police don't have much evidence against me, Lena. There's the security video from the Lakes' apartment. You'll need a copy from Oldenberg, and you can have it examined, go through it carefully. You might be able to prove it's been edited."

"Right, Nat. I'm going to try and get you out on bail, but I don't know if they'll agree. By the way, has Oldenberg got something against you?" Lena asked.

"We used to be colleagues in the NYPD. He didn't think my jokes were funny."

"The famous Marley sense of humor? That's got you into trouble before. I'll see you in the morning."

I was left alone in my cell. My last visitor that night was Oldenberg. He looked happier than ever.

"No questions without my lawyer present, Oldenberg."

"I only wanted to wish you good night, Marley. You got everything you need? You feeling comfortable?"

"I'll remember you in my dreams, Oldenberg."

*   *   *

I didn't get much sleep that night. The events of the last three days kept going around in my head. My only hope was that Lena could find some evidence on the security video. I had no appetite; I left my breakfast untouched. And I don't recommend NYPD coffee.

Lena was at Police Headquarters by nine o'clock in the morning. I was taken to an interview room to see her. She'd had the film from Lake's security video examined carefully.

"It's not looking good, Nat." Lena said. "Whoever edited this did a very good job. Black and white security film isn't great quality to start with. It makes it easier to hide any editing."

"This is becoming one long nightmare, Lena."

"I know, Nat. I've got one of our investigators looking into Robert and Angela Lake and the Lake Software Corporation."

"You know why their stock price is going down?" I asked.

"I know the story. Something about a new product nobody wants to buy."

I also told Lena what I had learnt from conversations with Lake and Tommy Lam. "If the corporation is in real deep trouble, it could explain a lot," I continued. "Such as Robert Lake's behavior. It's so extreme. He's not acting the safe respectable boss; he's playing a dangerous game, using Lam's professional services."

Oldenberg arrived to interview me. "I hope you slept well, Marley. Are our cells comfortable enough?" he asked.

"Couldn't be better. I didn't have to pay a cent. A single room with room service. That's two hundred dollars minimum uptown. I'm saving cash every minute I'm here. Thanks."

"Cut it out, Marley. We're going to start." Oldenberg put a fresh tape in the cassette recorder.

"Interview with Mr. Nathan Marley. Date: Friday, December 23rd. Time: 9:30 AM. Officers present: Captain Oldenberg and Lieutenant Brandstein. Also present: Ms. Lena Rosenthal, lawyer for Mr. Marley."

Oldenberg relaxed and smiled, and rubbed his hands. He was a very cheerful man.

"Mr. Marley, were you in McFadden's Bar about seven-thirty on the evening of 19th December?"

"Yeah. So what? I usually am," I answered.

"Just a simple 'Yes' or 'No,' if you please. Did you see this woman enter the bar?" Oldenberg asked and handed me a photo of Angela Lake.

"Uh-huh. That's her," I said.

"What did you notice about her?"

"Expensively dressed. Blonde hair, diamond necklace, earrings. Short black dress. Looked as if she had something on her mind."

"Can you describe what happened in the bar?"

"I was watching from my table. She ordered a drink and lit a cigarette. Then she took a letter out of her purse. Her face changed. Looked really upset. Threw a hundred-dollar bill on the bar. Didn't wait for change and rushed out."

"And you followed her out?"

"Yeah. I was curious. I thought she was deliberately trying to attract attention. I'd finished my drink and didn't have anything better to do that night. I wanted to see where she was going, what she was doing."

"I suggest you were attracted by her jewelry and the money she was throwing around. You decided to attack her."

Lena immediately stopped him. "Captain Oldenberg! I object to this line of questioning. My client did no such thing. In future, please keep to facts."

Oldenberg didn't look pleased. "All right, Ms. Rosenthal, I take that back. Mr. Marley, could you describe what happened after you left McFadden's Bar?"

"Mrs. Lake ran across Second Avenue just before the lights changed. I could see her walking along 42nd Street toward Grand Central. I followed but I couldn't get close. Then I lost her in the crowds at Grand Central. Had a couple more beers back at the bar. Went home. Woke up the next morning with a headache. End of story."

"You say Mrs. Lake was at your office the next morning," Oldenberg continued.

"She was there. Wanted to speak to me."

"Strange, because that morning Mrs. Lake was at her desk at Lake Software. She says she's never been near your office." Oldenberg looked pleased with himself.

"She's lying. She was there, and I can prove it – " I began.

Suddenly there was a loud knock at the door.

"Interview stopped at 9:50 AM," said Oldenberg, who turned off the cassette recorder. A sergeant entered.

"Sergeant, this had better be important. We're in the middle of an interview."

"It is important, sir. Mr. and Mrs. Lake are at reception. They want to speak to you, sir, in person. It's urgent."

"OK, Sergeant. I'll go. Everybody stay where you are. Sergeant, some coffee for our guests. I won't be a minute."

Oldenberg's minute stretched to forty-five minutes. We sat there in silence. You don't feel like making conversation in an interview room. Finally, Oldenberg returned. Now, he looked furious. He switched on the cassette recorder and said simply, "Interview finished at 10:35 AM."

"What do you mean 'interview finished?'" I asked.

"Marley, you can go. Go on, get out! Don't come back. No, never come back," said Oldenberg.

Lena was furious. "Captain Oldenberg! That is no way to talk to a respectable citizen of this city. My client needs both an apology and a full explanation," she demanded.

"All right. The NYPD wishes to apologize to you, Mr. Marley. All charges against you will be dropped."

I enjoyed that. The first time I'd heard him apologize to anybody.

Oldenberg continued, "According to the Lakes, this has all been a misunderstanding, a terrible mistake. Mrs. Lake says she has a bad memory for faces. Says she can't be sure who mugged her. Strange, that. She was sure enough yesterday. Mr. Lake says there a problem with the security cameras and has just given me a film that shows him hitting Mr. Marley first. He says it was just a friendly fight. No hard feelings."

Lena was now very angry. "Captain Oldenberg, I will be making a complaint to the authorities. My client has been wrongfully arrested. He has suffered in many ways. And as for the Lakes – "

"Ms. Rosenthal, I hear you," said Oldenberg. "Who knows what the Lakes are playing at? I've had ten officers on this case. A lot of valuable man-hours. You'll be pleased to know I've arrested the Lakes for making a false report. They're cooling off in the cells now. I'll enjoy questioning them. And Marley, between you and me, I dislike people who waste police time a lot more than I dislike private eyes."

"Thanks, Oldenberg. Give the Lakes a hard time," I said.

"I promise. Don't leave town, Marley. I'll need your help. I want to see the Lakes in jail."

"Like any good citizen, it's my duty and pleasure to help the NYPD."

Chapter 10   *General Post Office*

Another cold, gray morning but it felt good to be free, breathing the clean fresh air coming in off the East River. Lena and I walked across Police Plaza. A black stretch limo was parked on the other side of the Plaza. I'd seen the car before. Freedom wasn't going to last long. One of Tommy Lam's bodyguards called.

"Mr. Marley? Mr. Lam would like to talk."

"Give me two minutes," I said.

"Sure, Mister."

I turned to Lena. "This business isn't finished yet. That's Tommy Lam over there. The Lakes are good at making enemies and Tommy Lam's one of them. As for Robert Lake, he seems to be looking for that extra excitement in reaching the top in business. He's going to get his fingers burned badly. He might think differently after a few hours with Oldenberg."

"You're going to get in that car?" asked Lena.

"I don't have a choice. Keep this for me, will you?"

I turned my back on Lam and handed Lena my wallet. "Put it in your purse, quick! I can't explain now," I said.

"Take care, Nat."

"Trust me. And call Stella."

I climbed into the limo again. The bodyguards sat along the back seat, like a couple of statues. This morning there was a huge pink diamond in Lam's tiepin.

"A drink, Mr. Marley?" offered Lam.

"Thanks. Make it a large one. I need to get rid of the taste of police interview room."

"As I said yesterday, my assistants have methods of persuading people," said Lam.

The bodyguards grinned. I started to feel nervous.

"There's something about a knife," said Lam. "The ideal weapon if you want to really frighten someone. You see, we paid the Lakes a visit early this morning. Five is always the best time. We let ourselves in. A little surprise for them."

"Sure. I expect the Lakes offered you breakfast?" I said.

"They were a little confused." Lam continued. "I explained the reason for my visit. I was looking after my business interests. The Lakes didn't realize that if you went to prison, my payment could be in danger. You have some property of the Lakes. A diamond necklace and a pair of earrings, perhaps? I consider that my property now. I don't think the police will be watching the Parcel Room now. A perfect opportunity."

"So you asked the Lakes to change their stories?" I said.

"Very soon after my assistants offered to change Mrs. Lake's appearance . . . Now, there's another matter I'd like to discuss. But first, another drink?"

I hadn't eaten any breakfast and the Scotch was going straight to my head. I'd have to be careful.

"Not now, thanks, Mr. Lam."

"Naturally, I don't wish to use my methods on you."

"Very kind, I'm sure."

"Not kind, just practical. I dislike violence," said Lam.

We'd been traveling uptown on Sixth Avenue for some

time. The car turned left on to 34th Street, then continued across town. I knew where we were heading.

"Another visit to the Post Office, Mr. Lam?"

"Of course. Now, Mr. Marley, before we get there, I'd like to ask you about the diamond necklace that Mrs. Lake says she hid in your office."

I knew I had to play for time. I hadn't told Lam any lies. I kept quiet.

"You know the necklace I mean?" Lam continued. "Mrs. Lake was wearing it in McFadden's Bar."

"Sure, I know. A lot of rocks," I said.

"Easily worth five hundred thousand dollars. Where is it, Marley?"

He had stopped saying "Mister." He was getting serious.

"I don't know anything about a diamond necklace. The police have been all over my office and didn't find anything."

"Either you are lying or Mrs. Lake is. I suspect you are. Mrs. Lake was too frightened to say anything but the truth. But don't worry, I'll find out."

The car had arrived at the back of the General Post Office on Ninth. Inside General Delivery, that day's crowd of homeless and down-and-outs were waiting in two lines. Some guys carried large black plastic bags with all their possessions. Some were coughing terribly. It was painful to listen. How could anybody sleep on the streets of Manhattan in December?

This time Lam behaved. He waited patiently in the line until we got to the window.

"Anything for Marley?" I asked.

"Initial?" asked the clerk.

"*N* for Nathan."

"Here we are, two packages. Sorry, your ID."

I searched my pockets. "That's strange," I said. "I had my wallet at Police Headquarters. Maybe I dropped it."

"No ID, no packages," said the clerk.

Lam lost control. He banged on the window and shouted at the clerk. "You *know* who he is! You checked his ID yesterday."

"I repeat. No ID, no letter. U.S. Post Office rules," said the clerk.

Lam banged again on the window. "Damn it, woman! Are you stupid?" The bodyguards joined in, shouting at the clerk. They weren't making themselves popular. Some guys waiting in the lines didn't take kindly to rich well-fed guys in smart suits being rude to their Post Office clerk.

"Hey, stop that, man! Get out of here!"

"What do you guys want? You don't belong here."

A tall black guy went up to Tommy Lam and pushed him hard in the face. Lam wasn't used to being pushed around. He was furious.

"Fix him, boys!" shouted Lam.

The bodyguards smiled and started to beat up the black guy. It didn't last long. Twenty angry guys against two bodyguards. Those Armani suits didn't look smart any more. Especially with big guys standing on them. Seconds later, the Post Office Police crashed into the room.

"Police! Raise your hands! Face the wall!"

The clerk had set off the alarm. I was very glad to see those officers, but I had to act quickly. I spoke to the sergeant.

"The name's Marley, licensed private investigator. These

men are holding me by force. They're trying to steal packages sent to me at General Delivery. I need to speak to Captain Oldenberg at Police Headquarters immediately."

Stealing U.S. mail is a serious crime. The Post Office Police took me seriously as well. The sergeant pointed at Lam and company. "Lock those guys up, boys," he ordered. "Now, Mr. Marley, let's make that call."

*   *   *

The Post Office Police kept Lam and his bodyguards, and me in separate rooms at the Post Office. I didn't like the idea of sharing a room with Lam's assistants. The clerk had seen enough of the situation to recognize that I wasn't with Lam out of choice. Telephone calls were made to Oldenberg and Lena Rosenthal.

Oldenberg looked cheerful when he arrived. I could see he'd had a good morning.

"I've charged the Lakes with making a false report. That's a serious crime," said Oldenberg.

"You're going to enjoy talking to the mysterious Mr. Lam," I said.

"The guy who goes by the name Tommy? We know something about him. We've had him in for questioning several times but never had enough evidence to charge him with anything. He has a business called Shanghai Computer Commerce. The strange thing is, when you get to his place, it's just a tiny office above a restaurant, full of the latest computer equipment. He says his business is 'buying and selling.' That could mean anything."

"Brings in enough to pay for the limo, driver, bodyguards and diamond tiepins," I said.

Lena arrived with my wallet and ID.

"I'm glad you're safe, Nat. Is Lam safely locked up, Captain?" she asked.

"He is for the moment. I don't know how long we'll be able to hold him. I think Lam's the key to this affair. I'd like to see what he does when we let him out."

"He's frightened the Lakes," I said. "And I don't mind if he frightens them some more."

General Delivery was opened especially for us. The clerk handed over two small packages, both addressed to Mr. N. Marley. The first one contained Angela Lake's claim ticket and briefcase key. The other one contained the diamond necklace.

"Will you look at that!" said Oldenberg, his eyes wide with surprise.

"That's just part of what Tommy Lam's looking for," I said. "There should be more at the Grand Central Parcel Room. Lam would love to get his hands on it. From what I understand, Lake has been late in paying for Lam's professional services. Lam's just collecting what he's owed in his own sweet way."

"Where did Mrs. Lake leave the necklace?" asked Oldenberg.

"Stella found it in the filing cabinet and hid it in her blouse while your boys were searching my office."

Oldenberg laughed. "The one place they didn't look. The Lakes thought they had set you up perfectly. OK, I'll have the Post Office Police hold Lam until we get back from Grand Central. I want to see what's inside that briefcase first."

The patrol car took Oldenberg, Lena, and me uptown to 42nd Street.

"You know what, Oldenberg?" I said. "We haven't gotten to the bottom of this affair."

"What do you mean?" asked Oldenberg.

"I don't think the Lakes have told you everything. According to Tommy Lam, they hired him to hack into the Osaka Net development center. Not standard business practice for any respectable organization. That's one part of it. The other is why did they want me to be their fall guy? What's the motive behind that?"

"I could suggest something," said Lena. "If Lake Software is in as deep trouble as the newspapers are suggesting, perhaps the Lakes are trying to make money from anything they've got which isn't tied up with the business. I wonder if the Lakes were planning to make an insurance claim on the jewelry. They could have sold off most of the jewelry before trying to set you up. Then they could say that you had sold everything after robbing Mrs. Lake."

"They'd have to be desperate if they imagined that trick would succeed," said Oldenberg.

We went down to the Parcel Room on the lower level at Grand Central. I'd seen the clerk before when I'd gone to collect my empty briefcase. I could see recognition in his eyes. He looked alarmed. "Not you again," he said.

"Relax," said Oldenberg. "He's harmless. We arrested the wrong guy."

The clerk handed over Angela Lake's briefcase. I unlocked it and opened it. Inside there was another surprise for us: it was empty except for a pair of earrings. The same earrings I'd seen her wearing in McFadden's.

"The question is, where's the rest of the stuff?" asked Lena.

"If those two photos that Angela Lake showed me were real, then the Lakes have gotten rid of a lot of rocks," I said. "The Lakes could have said that I had sold everything except those earrings after mugging Angela."

Oldenberg was thinking hard. "I've got it, Marley. If I let the Lakes and Lam and his boys out, we should find out what's happening. I can hold them all till tomorrow. I've already got a list of crimes I could charge Lam with, but that's not enough. I want the big one. We'll check this briefcase back in the Parcel Room and give the claim ticket and key back to Mrs. Lake. I'll tell Lam that I've returned Mrs. Lake's property to her. I'll also tell him I've kept the necklace as evidence. Then we wait for the fun to start."

"I'd love to see Lam's face when you tell him you've got the necklace," I said.

"He's going to be furious," replied Oldenberg. "And when he finds out there's only a pair of earrings in the briefcase . . . Lam won't harm you now, Marley. Relax and get a good night's sleep. I'll be in touch."

Chapter 11 *A call from Oldenberg*

Christmas Eve morning. I woke up early feeling on top of the world. Even Queens looked attractive in the pale winter sunshine. I'd gone right home after lunch the previous day and just slept and slept. It was time for breakfast at Slim Pete's Diner down the street.

"Good morning, Pete. It's great to see you and just great to be alive. Merry Christmas!"

"What's wrong with you, Nat?" asked Pete. "Why aren't you miserable as usual?"

"I've just escaped a ten-year jail sentence."

"Oh. Is that all? They should've locked you up and thrown away the key," Pete joked.

"You sure know how to please your customers. A breakfast special. And a big sweet smile if you can remember how to do one," I said.

After breakfast, I caught the number seven train to Grand Central. Midtown Manhattan seemed more of a madhouse than usual, with crowds of shoppers desperately searching for last-minute presents. That reminded me. I still hadn't bought any. One look inside Macy's and I decided against it. There's nothing worse than a New York department store on Christmas Eve. I didn't get to the office until ten.

"Morning, Nat. Feeling OK?" asked Stella.

"Couldn't be better," I replied.

"There's someone waiting in your office. Just arrived."

I stepped through into my office. There was a middle-aged man sitting in the client's chair. Large and overweight, and wearing an awful brown suit. It was Oldenberg.

"Captain Oldenberg! What can I do for you on this beautiful morning?"

"Morning, Marley. I wanted to talk some more about our friends, the Lakes."

"And Tommy Lam?"

"Yeah. I'll get on to him in a minute. I was thinking about the interview with the Lakes. At first we didn't get anywhere. They just kept saying, 'Oh, what a terrible mistake' and, 'So sorry for wasting your time.' Then it got more interesting."

"Go on," I said.

"Robert Lake is the strangest character I've met for some time. By the way, I liked the damage you did to his nose."

I examined my right hand. "I sure hope it hurt him more than it hurt me," I said.

"Lake seems to be deeply bored with life," continued Oldenberg. "Maybe he's spent too long developing computer software. The papers are full of stories about Lake Software. The stock price is still falling. Lake ought to be a very worried man. That's what I can't figure out – he doesn't seem to be at all worried. I couldn't get much sense out of him. What the Lakes did to you is very serious. They could get ten years in jail for trying to set you up. But all he said was, 'We lost that one. We didn't play our cards right.' He's not admitting to any connection with Tommy Lam."

He paused for a moment and then continued, "Angela

Lake's scared, but she's still trying to be as cool as possible. It was like questioning the ice queen. I got some sense out of her, though. She's standing by her husband, but that early-morning visit from Lam has made her think. Wonder how long she'll remain faithful. By the way, she's asked for police protection."

"You didn't give it to her?"

"No way, Marley. I want to see what happens. Either Robert Lake or Lam is going to make a move and I intend to be there when it happens. You should have seen Lam's face when I told him the diamond necklace was now police evidence."

"So what now, Oldenberg?"

"We wait and see. Lam knows that I've returned the claim ticket and key to Angela Lake. I want to see the three of them behind bars. But we need more evidence. This is the plan. We released the Lakes and Lam and his boys first thing this morning, and now we have them all under surveillance. I'm going to make sure every one of them is put away for a long long time."

If I was in Robert Lake's shoes I'd be terrified. He'd said he enjoyed taking chances and going for the big one. Oldenberg said he wasn't at all nervous. Just as well. You'd need to be made of iron to play against Tommy Lam. I just felt glad to be out of it. Lam and the Lakes had all caused me more than enough trouble but thankfully they weren't my responsibility now.

I needed to talk to Lena Rosenthal so I decided to take a walk downtown. Outside it was still below freezing. There were heavy snow clouds in the sky. A homeless woman was lying in a shop doorway, on a bed made out of dirty blankets and cardboard boxes. I put ten dollars in the plastic cup she was holding out.

It took about ten minutes to get to Lena's office on East 34th and Lexington Avenue. As I arrived, the first snowflakes were beginning to fall.

"Nat, how are you feeling? Still in one piece after a night at Police Headquarters?" asked Lena.

"I'm fine. Amazing what fifteen hours' sleep can do."

Lena brought me up-to-date with what she had discovered. She had suspected the Lakes might have made a big insurance claim. In fact, such a claim had been made with Pacific Central Insurance for ten million dollars in stolen jewelry, including the diamond necklace. Insurance companies never like paying out money, and Pacific Central thought losing all that jewelry was just a bit too careless. But that claim might just have succeeded if I had been less suspicious and believed Angela Lake.

"Now that reminds me, Nat," said Lena. "Our investigator went into the Lakes' past histories. This should interest you."

Lena handed me a color copy of a magazine article with a picture of a group of students standing beneath the Washington Square Arch. The headline read: "New Star At Performing Arts Festival." Lena had marked the sentence: "Angela Webster stars as Kate in Oklahoma State University's production of the classic Cole Porter musical *Kiss Me Kate* – the 'must-see show' of this year's festival." In the center of the group was Angela Webster, now Lake, with wavy brown hair.

"Will you look at that!" I said. "Not only is Angela

Lake not a blonde, she's not from Coney Island either. Anyway, this proves one thing: she's a good actress. Maybe she needed those acting skills when she married Robert Lake's money."

As I left the building I started thinking about what I had been through in the last few days. I'd been arrested for robbery. I'd spent a night at Police Headquarters. Then I'd been released, and Captain Oldenberg had started being pleasant to me. Maybe it was time my life went back to normal.

But I had been back in the office only five minutes before Stella put a call through. It was Oldenberg.

"Marley? It's happened. Tommy Lam has made the first move. Angela Lake has been kidnapped and Lam's got the claim ticket."

"When?" I asked.

"Eleven o'clock this morning. He met her outside the Lakes' apartment. The doorman saw everything. Lam spoke to her briefly and she got in his car."

"Yeah? If it's one of Tommy Lam's invitations, you don't refuse."

"Then my boys followed them downtown to Grand Central. One of Lam's bodyguards picked up the briefcase from the Parcel Room and returned it to Lam's car. Then they managed to lose them in the midtown traffic. I should have done the job myself. But we know that Lam isn't pleased about what he found inside the briefcase. He phoned Robert Lake. He wants five million dollars in jewelry, cash, or both in exchange for his wife's safe return. And by the way, he told Lake not to speak to the police."

"But you know everything?" I asked.

"Lake seems to be coming to his senses. He called me immediately," replied Oldenberg.

"I wish you good luck with our Mr. Lam."

"Sorry, Marley, but this isn't the end of the story for you. Lam wants a go-between to take messages between him and Lake. He told Lake that he would only speak to you. He says you're a professional and the only guy he can trust. We're going to pay Robert Lake a visit at his apartment. I'll pick you up in five minutes."

I'd had enough of Lam and the Lakes and anything connected with them. But like it or not, I was involved again. I explained to Stella what had happened.

"I don't like it, Nat," she said.

"Neither do I. Another opportunity for me to play the good citizen."

Chapter 12   *An appointment with Lam*

Now the snow was falling more heavily as the police car made its way slowly uptown on Madison Avenue to 86th Street. The subway would have been quicker, but police captains don't take the subway.

Inside the lobby at the Lakes' apartment building everything was much the same as it had been on my last visit. Except this time the doorman wasn't smiling unpleasantly. They needed me now. Oldenberg and I were shown into Robert Lake's office. There was a new carpet on the floor. It must have been difficult to clean off the blood. I was trying to calculate what they'd spent on carpets when Lake's personal assistant entered. She was the perfect host.

"Captain Oldenberg and Mr. Marley, do take a seat. Mr. Lake's expecting you. Can I get you anything?"

"Espresso coffee and a large Scotch," I said.

"Just coffee for me," said Oldenberg.

The assistant went into the next room. A moment later a door opened and Robert Lake entered. This time he was wearing round glasses. There was a bandage over his nose and bruising on his face. I admired my work. Lake gave a faint smile. "Gentlemen, thank you for coming. Please excuse me. I am exhausted and suffering stress."

"That's nothing to the stress you caused me, buddy," I shouted. "You could begin by apologizing."

Oldenberg was nervous. "Marley, this isn't the time – "

"If this isn't the time, what damn time is, then?" I pointed a finger in Lake's face. "Never play games with me again! Thanks to you I was nearly sent to jail. I've got Tommy Lam to thank for the fact that I'm free. Now I don't know who the bigger rat is – you or Lam. I won't do anything for you until I get an apology."

"Marley, go easy," warned Oldenberg.

"A proper apology!" I shouted.

At last, Lake spoke. "You're right, Mr. Marley. You should have an apology. I am sincerely sorry for all that I have done, and I will do everything possible to put right the wrongs that I have caused you."

"Thank you." That made me feel a whole lot better.

We got down to business over coffee. "Tell Marley what happened this morning," said Oldenberg.

Lake was no longer the self-confident little man. In a low quiet voice he retold the events of the morning, and how he had received a demand from Lam for five million dollars in cash, jewelry, or both.

"I thought I had everything under control. It didn't work out," said Lake.

"Too late for self-pity, Lake. It's a rough tough world out there," I said. Then I turned to Oldenberg. "We've got to act carefully. You took a chance coming here. We don't want Lam to know the police are involved."

"So who's in charge of this case, you or me, Marley?" demanded Oldenberg.

"If I have to be the go-between, I do things my way, not your way. Understood?" I said.

"OK, OK. Understood."

"What happens next?" I asked Lake.

"Lam will call with further instructions. He wants to talk."

"I thought he might. I trust you have the payment, Lake?"

"Of course. My corporation is a major software developer."

"That's not what the *Wall Street Journal* is saying."

Lake didn't like that. "I don't need reminding, Mr. Marley. I shall pay Mr. Lam the full amount in jewelry," he said.

"OK. This time I'm making the rules," I said. "These are my conditions, Lake. You have to be totally honest with me. You tell me everything. Do exactly as I say at all times. Don't think, don't make decisions. I do that. Can you have the jewelry here this afternoon?"

"Yes."

"So where is it now? We'd expected to find it in the briefcase at Grand Central."

"At the Chase Manhattan Bank on Fifth Avenue. But the police have the diamond necklace."

"I need all the jewelry here. We may have to be ready to move quickly. Oldenberg, can you get the necklace here this afternoon? Have a plainclothes officer bring it."

"I'll see to it," said Oldenberg.

"And Oldenberg, I don't want to see uniformed officers near this building. And everybody, no decisions without asking me first."

Lake's assistant came in while we were talking. "Mr. Lam is on the phone. Wants to speak to Mr. Marley personally."

I picked up the phone on Lake's desk. "Marley speaking."

"Listen carefully. Leave the building. Go across to the 86th Street subway station. Take any downtown train." The line went dead.

"I've been told to take a ride on the subway," I said.

"I'll have a couple of my boys follow you," said Oldenberg.

"I'm in charge. I do this alone or not at all."

I didn't know what to expect on the subway. I sat in a center car and waited. The train sped downtown. 77th Street, 68th, 59th. At 42nd, crowds of people with their Christmas shopping poured into the car. It was standing room only. I gave up my seat to a tired-looking mother with two crying children. Someone crashed into me and pushed through to the next car.

"Watch where you're going, buddy!" I shouted.

I looked down. There was a piece of paper sticking out of my coat pocket. The note read: "Get off at 14th Street – Union Square. Take a cross-town L train to 14th Street and Eighth Avenue."

I did as I was told and changed trains. I sat there reading the public health information notices in English and Spanish on the walls of the car. The L train had reached the end of the line but I hadn't gotten any more instructions yet. All I could do was get off. Another guy crashed into me and rushed off without apologizing. I was beginning to feel like a punching bag in a gym. Another piece of paper was sticking out of my coat pocket. It read simply: "Walk west along 14th Street."

Manhattan changes so quickly. I was now just below the Chelsea area. Not a skyscraper anywhere. Plenty of traditional New York brownstone houses. Five or six floors with fire escapes on the fronts of the buildings. The neighborhood was full of little bars, restaurants, and stores. As I walked toward the Hudson River waterfront, it changed yet again. Parking lots and factories, some working, some empty. The snow was falling steadily. It made everywhere peaceful and quiet. That felt strange in Manhattan.

I was almost at the end of 14th Street. I could see the river across Tenth and Eleventh Avenues. I didn't have time to admire the view of New Jersey in the distance. A black stretch limo had stopped in front of me. The windows were as black as the paint. The car looked as inviting as an NYPD cell. A back window was lowered slightly. I was ordered to get in.

Chapter 13   *The deal*

Inside the car, the two bodyguards sat like statues along the back seat. Tommy Lam looked very relaxed. Another morning, another tiepin, with the largest white diamond I'd ever seen a man wearing.

"Good afternoon, Mr. Marley. So pleased you could come. A drink?" Lam offered.

"I don't feel like drinking," I replied.

"Marley, people who refuse me are either very brave or very foolish."

"Let's just say I don't like guys who drive around Manhattan in stretch limos," I said.

"That's not very polite of you."

"I'm not here to be polite, Lam."

We had already stopped calling each other "Mister." I knew the meeting would be short and businesslike.

"Then we understand each other, Marley," said Lam. "I asked for you because you're a professional. The Lakes are amateurs. I need someone like you to keep Robert Lake under control. He's the problem."

"I don't trust him," I said. "And I don't really care what happens to him."

"Agreed, but he's still necessary. A small matter of five million dollars. I need guarantees from your end, Marley. The first is the payment, in money or jewelry, or both. So far, I've only received a pair of earrings."

"Payment in jewelry will be ready this afternoon," I said.

"Good. The second is that the police will not be involved. I want them kept out of this. If I learn that the police are involved, my assistants will kill you and the Lakes."

The statues on the back seat came to life and grinned. They were looking forward to it. A murder would obviously make their Christmas merry.

"You've made yourself very clear, Lam. I also need a guarantee from you. Is Angela Lake safe and well?"

Lam passed me a videotape.

"Play that tape to Lake when you return to the Lakes' apartment. You will see that Mrs. Lake is well. Mrs. Lake also has a message that her husband should hear. I think he'll enjoy the show." The bodyguards smiled again.

"After you have seen Lake again, go home and have a good night's sleep. Report to the Lakes' apartment by nine tomorrow morning." Lam handed me a cell phone. "You will receive a call on this phone. Make sure you have a car and driver ready. And have the payment and Robert Lake with you or the deal is off."

Lam's car had been heading uptown on Amsterdam Avenue. It came to a stop just behind Lincoln Center. Lam pointed at the door. Obviously his way of saying goodbye.

Working for Robert Lake had its advantages, though. I could now charge expenses. I started with a taxi across town. Of course, I'm a strong believer in public transport, but you tend not to believe in something so strongly when you're not paying for it. Central Park in the snow looked even more like a scene from a Christmas card.

That reminded me. I hadn't sent any Christmas cards. Never mind. People would understand. I usually forgot anyway.

The doorman couldn't have been more polite in the lobby at the Lakes' apartment. "Good afternoon, Mr. Marley, sir." I'm not used to being called "Mr. Marley, sir," but I didn't let it go to my head.

"I've spoken to Lam," I said to Lake. "He's given me his instructions. But first, there's the matter of my fee to sort out."

"But Mr. Marley – "

"Don't talk, Lake, just listen. When your lovely wife visited me at my office, she gave me two thousand dollars for my fee and expenses. That money found a good home at the South Bronx neighborhood center. I'll need a further five thousand for my fee and essential expenses. I want it in cash. And no thousand-dollar bills – bars really don't like changing them."

Lake said nothing but just nodded. Then he unlocked a drawer in his desk and pulled out a pile of bills. He counted out five thousand and handed it to me. Taking that money didn't make me feel proud of myself, but I had a business to run and rent to pay. The Lakes had already cost me more than enough in time and money.

"Now, have you got the payment for Lam ready?" I asked.

Lake removed a painting from the wall. Behind it was a wall safe, which he unlocked. He took out a briefcase and opened it. It was full of rocks. The diamond necklace that Oldenberg had returned lay on top of a pile of other jewelry. It all looked good.

"Lock it up for the night," I said. "I'm expecting a call here from Lam at nine tomorrow morning. When I get his instructions, you're coming with me. I want your car and driver ready."

"Why? Do I have to?"

"Lam insists. And if anything goes wrong, I know who to blame," I said.

"Mr. Marley, is my wife safe?"

"Well, aren't you just the perfect caring husband! I thought you'd never ask. I've got a video from Lam for you to watch."

The video was poor quality, but Angela Lake was there all right, sitting alone in a cheap hotel room. She spoke:

"Robert. I have a message for you from Mr. Lam. I'm fine. They're looking after me. Mr. Lam says to make sure there are no mistakes. Have all the jewelry with you. Follow the instructions exactly. He says to watch closely now."

Angela Lake was shaking. One of Lam's bodyguards pressed a knife against Angela's throat then took it away. For a moment there was a white mark where the metal had been pressed against her smooth skin. Lam was right. Knives are far more frightening than guns. Lake didn't react in any way. He just stared at the television.

"What are you going to do?" asked Lake.

"Nothing just now," I replied.

"I'm paying you five thousand dollars to – "

"Shut it! You disgust me. You're paying me five thousand bucks to think. Something that you're obviously not very good at. Make sure you're ready at eight-thirty tomorrow morning. I'm out of here."

Outside, the air smelt fresh, cold, and clean. I breathed in deeply.

*　　*　　*

I took a taxi back to East 43rd Street. More expenses to charge to Lake. I could have walked quicker. Any more snow and New York would come to a complete stop.

Stella gave me a warm welcome back at the office. "Nat, I'm so glad to see you. I was so worried."

"It was nothing much, Stella. Just another ride around town with Lam. Here's something more interesting. I got paid."

I spread the five thousand dollars out on the desk.

"Mmm! Now that's what I call interesting!" she said.

"And will you ask Joe to come over now. I'm meeting Tommy Lam tomorrow and I'm going to need backup."

"What's the deal with Lam?"

"I have to be at the Lakes' apartment tomorrow at nine to get instructions. From then on, I don't know how Lam wants to play it."

I had to make a call to Oldenberg. It wasn't to wish him a merry Christmas.

"Marley here. I've just left Robert Lake. Everything's ready for tomorrow. We just have to wait for Lam's instructions now."

"So where do we come in?" Oldenberg asked.

"I may be going on a mystery tour tomorrow to meet Lam, but I'm not going alone. I want backup."

"That's sensible," replied Oldenberg.

"I need three cell phones. One for me, one for the NYPD, and one for my colleague, Joe. I need them all set up so that no one else can listen in."

"No problem, Marley."

"And I want police backup, with unmarked cars. Have your people standing by anywhere at a safe distance. Let's say 90th and Fifth, from eight-thirty tomorrow morning."

"We'll be there."

"Sorry, Oldenberg. Does this mean you won't be able to enjoy Christmas in the warmth and comfort of your family?"

"No problem. With my three teenagers, it'll be a pleasure to be out of the house. Marley, you'll have all the backup you need. The equipment will be with you in an hour. I'll send someone to set it all up for you."

Half an hour later, Joe arrived. I explained the situation.

"Joe, you still have those two guns at home, the Police Special and the shotgun?"

"Sure, boss. They haven't been fired in years, though."

"Clean the guns and bring them tomorrow."

"Don't you want a gun, boss?"

"No, you know I don't like carrying them. This is the plan. You'll have a cell phone to keep in touch with me. Then you'll be able to follow Lake's car. Keep well out of sight. There's not going to be much traffic tomorrow. When we stop for the meeting, try to get in close. I don't care how you do it. I want you to be around if things get nasty."

By that evening, the arrangements were made and we had full backup: Joe and the NYPD. It was almost time to relax. Time to spread a little Christmas cheer.

"Guys, it's Christmas Eve," I said. "We're going to be kind of busy tomorrow. Let's relax over some food. I'm taking you both out for dinner. I've got a table reserved at Smith and Wollensky's restaurant."

"Nat! You could say goodbye to five hundred bucks with the three of us eating there," exclaimed Stella.

"Correction, Stella. Lake Software will say goodbye to five hundred bucks. It's going to be on their expense account. Tonight, we're gonna enjoy ourselves – we've got a big day ahead of us tomorrow."

Chapter 14 *Christmas Day*

Christmas Day is the one day of the year when it's easy to take a car into Manhattan. No traffic jams and you can always find a parking space. I don't know why more people don't do it. The morning was cold and unpleasant, with freezing fog coming in off the East River. The side streets off the main avenues were still covered in the previous night's snow.

Robert Lake's car, a blue Mercedes, stood outside his apartment building with its engine running. Not good for the environment. But we'd be grateful for the warmth inside the car. I knew Joe and Oldenberg would be somewhere in the area waiting for us to move. I could depend on them to keep out of sight.

I went inside. Lake was waiting for me in the lobby with the briefcase. I quickly checked it over. Everything seemed to be in order. Now it was time to deal with Lake.

"Stand up and put your hands behind your back," I said.

"What the hell are you doing?" he demanded.

"Just do it before I have to get rough."

I tied his hands.

"What's all this? Am I some sort of criminal?" he asked.

"Yes, Lake, that's *exactly* what you are. Nothing personal. The less you can do, the better. I just feel safer with you under control."

The cell phone Lam had given me rang. Lam gave me brief instructions: "JFK Airport. Write this number . . . call me when you get close." Then the line went dead. I made a quick note, then pulled Lake outside.

"You and I are going to take a little ride," I said.

I put Lake in the back of the car and I sat with the driver. It wouldn't be comfortable for him tied up, but I didn't care. I gave the driver one hundred bucks and said to him, "It's too bad you have to work on Christmas Day. I hope this makes up for it. I'm in charge of this operation. You don't take any orders from Lake. Understood?"

"You're the boss, Mr. Marley," he said.

"First stop, JFK."

I relaxed in warmth and comfort. I held the briefcase tightly. It was all happening. I had the cell phone from Oldenberg in my pocket. If Joe and the NYPD didn't pick up the signal we'd be in deep trouble. The only thing I could do was cross my fingers and hope. The car made its way carefully through the deep snow and made a right onto Second Avenue. At least the main avenues were clear. I called Joe.

"Marley here. We're going downtown on Second, heading for JFK airport."

"We're behind you at a safe distance, boss," replied Joe.

"Receiving you loud and clear. Let's go," said Oldenberg.

We crossed the 59th Street Bridge over to Queens. The fog was growing thicker as we turned off Queens Boulevard onto Woodhaven Boulevard. Soon we were on Cross Bay Boulevard, approaching JFK. A few car lights appeared out of the fog from time to time. Probably families visiting relatives for Christmas lunch. I called my backup.

"We're on Cross Bay Boulevard," I said. "I don't want to see you guys anywhere near this car. Right?"

"You got it," said Joe.

"Relax, Marley. You're working with professionals," said Oldenberg.

I took out Lam's phone and punched in the number Lam had given me. "Where are you, Marley?" asked Lam.

"On Cross Bay Boulevard. Almost at JFK," I said.

"Keep going. Head for long-term parking. Call again when you're closer." The phone went quiet.

I called Joe and Oldenberg to tell them. JFK must be one of my least favorite areas of New York's five boroughs. The parking lots and airline terminals seem to go on for ever. Mile after mile of total ugliness. Once you arrive at JFK, you only want to do one thing – escape from it. The signs for the long-term parking lots started to appear. I called Lam's number again.

Lam said simply: "Parking Lot Seven."

I needed my backup. "Guys, it's Parking Lot Seven. I think this'll be the meeting point."

I had an immediate answer from Joe, but where was Oldenberg? If I couldn't get in touch with him, he would only have an rough idea where we were in this endless row of parking lots. I tried again and again. No success. Joe was with me, so no need to panic – yet. I told the driver to take his time. He had no choice but to take his time in the fog. Finally, we arrived at the entrance. There was something familiar about the guy who met us there. The only people I knew who wore dark glasses in the December snow were Lam's bodyguards. He told us to follow him across the lot. The place seemed to be completely empty.

Eventually, a black limo appeared and flashed its lights at us. Lam's guy told us to stop opposite it. If you had to die somewhere in New York City, an empty parking lot in JFK in December would be the worst place in the world you could wish for.

I sure hoped Joe could find us OK. If he was around, he was doing a good job of not showing it. Nothing seemed to be happening at Lam's end but you couldn't see a thing through the black windows of the limo. I opened a window slightly. The air was so cold it was painful to breathe. Tommy Lam stayed inside. He had planned everything very well. The middle of a huge parking lot. Nowhere to run to, nowhere to hide. But he hadn't planned for the fog.

*   *   *

How would Joe and the NYPD get me out of this one? The bodyguard came over and tapped on the window, signaling for me to get out. He searched me for weapons. I was clean. Then he spoke. I couldn't hear a word he said for the airplane noise.

"You'll have to speak up," I shouted.

"Mr. Lam wishes to know if you have the payment," said the bodyguard.

"I have everything Mr. Lam needs," I answered.

"I have instructions to take the payment to Mr. Lam."

"Not so fast, buddy. We do that. First, I need to know if Angela Lake is safe."

The bodyguard went back to Lam's car. There was a short conversation. I could see clouds of white breath in the freezing air. A minute later he returned.

"You will see Mrs. Lake very soon," he said.

The other bodyguard got out of the limo with Angela Lake. Apart from looking very angry, she seemed to be all right. In the distance, I could hear drunken singing, probably from a down-and-out. At least someone was enjoying himself on Christmas morning.

"Good," I said to the bodyguard. "I'll ask Lake to take the payment to Lam's car. One case full of jewelry. As soon as Lam has received payment, I expect the safe return of Mrs. Lake. But I want to see her standing next to Lam between the two cars before I send Lake over with the case."

The bodyguard returned to Lam's limo for another discussion. Meanwhile, I went around to the passenger door, took Lake outside and untied him. The experience of being tied up hadn't improved his language.

"You bastard, Marley. Why did you have to do that?" he demanded.

"I enjoy it. Now, listen, we don't do anything until we see your wife standing next to Lam. Then you hand over the case. Nice and slow. Just behave yourself."

Mrs. Lake was standing next to Lam, blowing on her hands to keep warm.

The bodyguard returned. "Mr. Lam is ready, Mr. Marley."

"I'm sending Lake over now," I said.

Lake got out and started walking toward Lam, carrying the case. I watched from behind a car door.

Through the fog, I could just make out a down-and-out, so drunk he could hardly stand. Joe's acting skills were perfect. He'd locked up enough drunks in his time with the NYPD.

Lam took the case from Lake, placed it on the ground and opened it. He appeared to be happy with the jewelry. The first thing he noticed was the diamond necklace. He held it up and called to his limo. A little bearded guy got out and hurried over. He fitted a jeweler's glass in his eye and examined the necklace closely. Then he grinned at Lam and handed it over. Lam looked at it almost as if he were in love with the thing. Then he nodded to the bodyguard who was holding Angela Lake. She was released and stood by her husband. They didn't look pleased to see each other again as they approached our car. Robert Lake just looked down at the ground while Angela Lake stared at her husband coldly.

By now, Joe was behind Lam's car. I could just hear singing above the noise of airplanes. I recognised the Christmas song, even though it was completely out of tune. Then there was the sound of breaking glass.

Lam was nervous. He looked at Joe appearing out of the fog and shouted to one of his bodyguards. "Victor, get that stupid drunk out of here!" One bodyguard left and walked over to Joe.

The jeweler was now sorting through the other stuff in the briefcase. But he wasn't smiling any more. His expression became serious, then angry. He shouted above the airplane noise.

"Mr. Lam, you got one nice diamond necklace, worth about half a million. The rest of the stuff isn't worth five hundred bucks."

"You sure?" asked Lam.

"Look, Mister, I've worked all my life on 47th Street. I know worthless rocks when I see them."

Lam and the other bodyguard stared furiously at the jeweler and the Lakes. I was looking somewhere else. Out of the corner of my eye I saw Joe bring a gun handle down sharply on the head of Victor. He fell to the ground unconscious. You couldn't hear anything except airplanes.

Lam, now furious, pointed at the Lakes. "I've had enough of working with amateurs. You two could never do anything right. I did a professional job for you when I hacked into Osaka Net. I trusted you, Lake, but you're not a man of honor. You don't deserve to live." He suddenly paused: "What's happened to Victor?"

Lam turned and saw his bodyguard lying unconscious in the snow. "What the hell's going on here?" he demanded. "Kill the Lakes and Marley."

Lam's remaining bodyguard had already lifted his gun when I heard the roar of a shotgun from behind me. The second bodyguard fell into the snow. Joe was now next to me and passed me an NYPD Police Special. Joe's gun was pointing at Lam.

"Drop the gun or you're next!" shouted Joe.

"You'd better think carefully," I said to Lam. "You don't have any choice now. We have two guns against your one. If you shoot first, you'll get one, maybe two of us. But I can promise you, you'll be dead. I've got an ex-NYPD marksman here who never misses. So ask yourself, 'Do I feel lucky?'" I'd always wanted to use that line.

Lam remained cool. "I'd rather be shot here than die in prison," he said.

He had a good point. Lam had nothing to lose now. Lam's driver and the jeweler didn't share the same opinion. The jeweler jumped into the car and they made their escape. They were doing the sensible thing.

"Drop the gun, Lam!" shouted Joe.

Lam ignored the order. He was a desperate man and in

that instant, I knew he would try to shoot us all if he could. I acted quickly. I threw myself to the ground, taking Angela Lake with me. Three shots. Two pistol shots from Lam were answered by a single shot from Joe. Lam lay lifeless in the snow. Angela Lake was lying across me and Robert Lake was lying face down. Angela got to her feet and pulled him up.

"Robert. Oh, my God! Speak to me," she screamed at him.

"Here, let me," I said. I pulled away his coat and jacket. Blood was covering his shirt. An entry and an exit wound. The bullet had passed through his shoulder. He was lucky. He'd probably live. His face was gray. I used the cell phone to call an ambulance and then turned to Angela Lake.

"Make yourself useful, Mrs. Lake," I said. "Help me get him into the back of the Mercedes . . . Now you've got to stop that bleeding. Keep him upright. Two pieces of material, anything will do. Press them hard against the entry and exit wounds, and keep them there. Do it now, if you want him to live."

Angela Lake followed my instructions without a word. I told the driver to start the engine to get some heat in the car. Robert Lake's eyes opened briefly.

"Mr. Marley? You're right. It's a rough tough world," said Lake.

"Don't talk," I said. "And Mrs. Lake, don't give him anything to drink."

I got out of the car and crossed over to Joe who was looking down at the bodies in the snow.

"What a way to spend Christmas, boss," said Joe. "I'll

have to stop working for you. It's getting kind of dangerous."

In the snow around Lam shone little flashes of brilliant color. The jewelry. The diamond necklace was still held tightly in Lam's hand, as if even in death he refused to let go of it. I pulled Lam's fingers apart and picked up the necklace. People say that diamonds are a girl's best friend. These diamonds hadn't won any friends. They'd just cost two lives. We checked the bodyguard who Joe had hit on the head. He was breathing.

Now there was a noise above the sound of airplanes. The scream of a police car. Our backup.

Chapter 15 *Presents*

Soon the NYPD car appeared out of the fog and parked by Lam's limo. Oldenberg got out and looked around with an surprised expression.

"Marley, you should stay clear of bad company," he said.

"It's a bad habit of mine. What took you so long?" I asked.

"Had a little trouble with this cell phone," explained Oldenberg. "Last thing we heard, you were approaching long-term parking. Then the line went dead. We checked with the airport authorities and found out there were two vacant parking lots. They seemed to be the most likely meeting points. We'd just checked out the first one when we heard the gunshots."

"I got some Christmas presents for you," I said. "I called an ambulance for Lake. He should live, and Angela Lake's OK. One of Lam's guys is unconscious. But as for Lam and this one . . . "

Oldenberg looked at the lifeless forms in the snow. "OK, Marley," said Oldenberg. "Give me the main points before I take the formal statements at Headquarters."

"Lam wanted the rocks as payment for the work he'd done for the Lakes – hacking into Osaka Net. If all had gone as planned maybe he'd be on a flight abroad by now. Most of the rocks were copies. The necklace was the only real item in the case. Lam brought a jeweler with him to check the stuff. When he realized they were copies, he was going to kill me and the Lakes." I handed Oldenberg the necklace. "Keep that safe. The rest of the stuff is worthless."

The ambulance arrived and Robert Lake and the unconscious bodyguard were taken away.

"Now," I said to Oldenberg, "I need a few answers from Angela Lake."

We got into the back of Lake's Mercedes where Angela Lake was sitting quietly. She looked shaken but kept herself under control. Oldenberg kept his mouth shut and let me run the show. I looked her straight in the eye and made sure I had her complete attention.

"Mrs. Lake, the reality is that you and your husband are going to jail for a long time. The only way you're going to shorten that sentence is to cooperate and make a full confession."

Angela looked at Oldenberg, almost as if she was doubting my word.

"Marley's right," said Oldenberg. "You're in deep enough trouble already. To start with there's the hacking operation. Then, you set up Marley to make it look as if he'd mugged you. Marley could have gone to prison instead of you."

Angela Lake nodded, took a deep breath and began. "Robert's a computer expert, but when it comes to business, I do all the thinking. Lam wouldn't wait for his money so we agreed to pay him in jewelry. It was my idea to set you up. It was the only way I could think of to get Lam off our backs."

"Yeah, yeah," I said quickly. "We know all that. Answer this one. Where are the other jewels? The real stuff?"

She paused for a moment, biting her lip. Then she said quietly: "We don't have them."

"Louder. I want to hear this," I said.

"We don't have them!" she shouted at me.

"Give me the full story," I said.

"The jewelry was one of the few things of value we owned," she began. "Everything else was rented, hired, or borrowed. I'd been quietly selling off the jewelry since November. I knew back then that the corporation could go under. I tried to turn everything possible into cash to pay off debts. I'd had perfect copies made of the jewelry so if I appeared in public, people wouldn't suspect. And if the NYPD had fallen for the story of the mugging, Lam would have been after you, and that would have given us some time. We were planning to get the insurance money and then disappear."

"So why not pay Lam off in cash? Why go through this performance with the jewelry if you knew the stuff wasn't real?" I demanded.

"I had no choice. The bank had frozen our accounts – corporate and personal. It isn't public knowledge yet. There aren't going to be any December salaries."

"So you tried to pull off one final trick. Did you seriously think a guy like Lam would have been taken in? Two people are lying out there dead. And it could just as easily be you lying there. You think you're so damn important that you can play around with people's lives."

Angela Lake sat in silence, looking down at her feet. Her eyes were full of tears. Pity for her would have been a waste of good feelings.

"You can do plenty more crying in Sing Sing," I said.

I still had the use of Lake's Mercedes. I suggested to Oldenberg that we could put Angela Lake in the NYPD car, and we could travel to Police Headquarters in more comfort.

"Police Plaza, driver," I said. "I'm sorry, but I don't reckon there'll be a job for you with Lake Software after Christmas."

"Just what I suspected, Mr. Marley," replied the driver. "I've got another job to go to."

"Is there a drink in this car?" I asked.

"There's a choice of Scotch in the mini bar."

Lake may not have known too much about the real world but he knew a good Scotch. As I poured out drinks for Joe, Oldenberg and myself, my hands started to shake. Delayed shock. You never think it affects you at the time but it always does. I phoned Stella.

"Hi, Stella. It's finished. I won't go into all the details now, but Joe and I are fine. So you can stop worrying and enjoy Christmas with your family."

The fog was now lifting, and the car drove quickly through the suburbs of Brooklyn. It wasn't long before we were crossing the Brooklyn Bridge into Manhattan, Lower East Side. For the first time that day, there were clear blue skies. The gray waters of the East River now shone golden in the pale sunshine. It felt good to be alive. At the beginning of the week, I'd had nothing to do. Now I'd had more than enough excitement. I wouldn't complain about divorce work or finding missing persons ever again.